The Beauty
Queen Killer

D1561700

*Also available in Perennial Library
by John Creasey:*

The Beauty Queen Killer

John Creasey

PERENNIAL LIBRARY

Harper & Row, Publishers, New York
Cambridge, Philadelphia, San Francisco, Washington
London, Mexico City, São Paulo, Singapore, Sydney

A hardcover edition of this book was originally published in England under the title *A Beauty for Inspector West*. A hardcover edition of *The Beauty Queen Killer* was published in the United States in 1954 by Harper & Brothers.

THE BEAUTY QUEEN KILLER. Copyright © 1954 by John Creasey. Copyright © renewed 1982 by Diana Creasey, Colin John Creasey, Martin John Creasey and Richard John Creasey. All rights reserved. Printed in the United States of America. No part of this book may be used or reproduced in any manner whatsoever without written permission except in the case of brief quotations embodied in critical articles and reviews. For information address Harper & Row, Publishers, Inc., 10 East 53rd Street, New York, N.Y. 10022. Published simultaneously in Canada by Fitzhenry & Whiteside Limited, Toronto.

First PERENNIAL LIBRARY edition published 1987.

Library of Congress Cataloging-in-Publication Data
Creasey, John.
   The beauty queen killer.
   Originally published under the title: A beauty for Inspector West.
   I. Title.
PR6005.R517B43   1987   823'.912   87-45031
ISBN 0-06-080887-X (pbk.)

87 88 89 90 91   OPM   10 9 8 7 6 5 4 3 2 1

The Beauty
Queen Killer

1

A Beauty Walks

"But listen, Betty," Harold Millsom said huskily, "it won't get you anywhere. It never does, in the long run. You'll regret it all your life, honestly you will."

"Darling," Betty said, "you just don't understand, that's all there is about it. I *must* go. Why, it's the opportunity of a lifetime! Hundreds, why thousands, of girls would give their right hands for my chance. Please don't make me unhappy about —about anything."

Millsom didn't answer, just looked at her as if he worshiped her beauty; and she was beautiful as few will ever be. So young, with great blue eyes and a skin without a blemish, a face which seemed to glow. As Millsom stared, it was as if her beauty made him suffer; tormented him. That showed in his eyes, in the way his lips tightened and twisted like those of a man in pain, determined not to break down.

"Honestly," Betty said solemnly, "I think I've got

1

everything, Harold—everything that matters to make me a star. I do, really."

"You little fool, you'll just be one of thousands who waste their lives prancing about the stage, making up to any oily old man who promises you a chance!" Millsom burst out. "The only chance you'll ever get will be sleeping—"

"Harold!"

Millsom gulped.

"Oh, I know," he muttered. "That was beastly. I'm sorry. I didn't really mean it, Betty, it's just that I hate to think of you being spoiled, ruined, disappointed, and you will be. That's what always happens."

"Don't be silly." Betty was tranquil again. "Some girls get to the top, don't they? What about Vivien Leigh and Jean Simmons, and all of them? They had to begin at the beginning, and that's what I'm doing. In fact, in some ways," Betty went on earnestly, "I've made a better start. I did win the competition, and—"

"I wish to God you'd never entered for the damned thing!"

"Oh, Harold, there you go again. It's no use, you know, and I'm sure you'll be the first to come and congratulate me when I'm a star."

Millsom moved suddenly, swiftly; startling her. But she was not afraid, for she had known him all her life, and had great trust in him. Even when his strong fingers gripped her shoulders and actually hurt, she wasn't afraid.

"Listen, you damned little idiot, you'll never be a star. They're fooling you. You can't act now, and you'll never be able to, it's past time someone stopped you from making a fool of yourself. They'll

2

just lead you up the garden and then throw you aside. You won't be worth a penny change when you're through."

"Harold," said Betty, very quietly, "you're hurting."

He didn't let her go, but shouted: "Are you going to listen to me? Are you?"

"Please let me go," Betty said, still quietly, "you're hurting."

He let her go.

He moved back a yard, staring, with the pain showing in his eyes again.

"I think I'd rather see you dead than ruined by that theater mob," he told her. "Listen, Betty, you must see reason. You've got a good job, and everything's fine. In a couple of years you and I could get married, even before that if you like. That's the kind of life you want, not kicking your legs in some third-rate chorus or buttering up some nasty old man who—"

"That's *quite* enough," Betty said.

She turned and walked away from him. She moved with a natural grace which was hurtful to him. Her back was toward him, but her face was engraved on his mind's eye; it was as if a part of himself was walking away.

He took an involuntary step forward.

"Betty!" he called, hoarsely.

She didn't look round.

He went forward again, but stopped. The ground of the Common rose slightly, and she was near the top of the rise, beauty outlined against a golden dusk, against dark clouds edged with burnished brass. To the right and the left were trees, oak and beech and birch, not far off was a children's playground, a little farther away were the bushes where young lovers were already moving, yearning for solitude. Beyond were the lanes across the Common, leading to the first of the little houses of this London suburb; houses built of yellow brick, darkened by the passing years, yet looking bright and fresh and almost new in this clear evening light, which would fade when the glistening brass edges of the clouds rolled away.

They were dark clouds.

Betty moved toward the houses, along the gravel pathway, past the children's playground and its shrieking, shouting crowds, past a Common keeper, who touched his peaked cap and then stood and stared after her. So did three youths who had just come onto the Common. One of them gave a wolf whistle. Harold Millsom heard that, and his hands clenched, his face went very white.

He took another step forward, glaring at the youths, who were a hundred yards away.

"Take it easy, Harold," a man said, from behind him.

Millsom spun round.

A tall, thin man with a long neck and a large Adam's apple stood near some bushes. Millsom and Betty had been close to them; this man might have been there all the time, and heard everything. Every word.

"What the hell are you doing there, Tick?" Millsom was so angry, so deeply hurt, that he would gladly strike anyone, do anything to get release from the tension. "Come on, tell me, how long you been there?"

"Take it easy, old lad," Tick said hastily, "it's a public place, isn't it? I've got every right—"

4

"How long have you been there?" Millsom's voice grew shrill.

"Not long, and I never did any harm, chum. Why don't you unwind a bit, old boy, go on the loose—like Betty?" He gave a quick, nervous, hopeful grin. "That's what you want to do. No use losing your loaf, is there? She'll come back when she's proved you're right—"

"So you've been there all the time, have you?" Millsom said unsteadily. "Why, you dirty, sneaking Peeping Tom, I'll smash your face in."

"Keep away!" Tick gasped, in sudden alarm, and flung his arms up in a futile flurry of defense.

It was no more than a gesture.

Powerful fists smacked into his face, his stomach, his chest; he felt one eye close, tasted the salt of blood on his lips, gasped and cried and gave ground fast, but could not get away from the savage, vicious, pounding fists.

He was just a heap on the ground when Millsom walked blindly away, and three youths, one of whom had whistled after Betty, watched him as they hurried to see what had happened to Tick.

Tick was sobbing, bleeding, blinded by tears and blood.

Betty closed the door of one of the little houses, an hour later, and walked toward the Common. It was dark but for the street lamps. She didn't really like the thought of crossing the Common, but it offered a short cut to the main road and the buses for the half-hour ride to the West End. She walked quickly, and no one followed her.

She wasn't likely to have any more bother with Harold, she persuaded herself. She was sorry, but he simply didn't understand. If he had his way she would marry him now, and they would settle down to a little house and a lot of kids. He'd often hinted that he'd like a big family, and where would that get them? The pictures twice a week, perhaps, and the pools, and her figure would be ruined in a few years. Kids did that to your figure, didn't they? Oh, no, that wasn't the life for her, the Beauty Queen of South London with a small part in a British film almost certain, and goodness knew what to follow. She was confident of her ability, and that caused the trouble—at home as well as with Harold, no one had any faith in her.

She could see the greenish glow of the big main-road lights from the top of the hill. This was near the spot where she had talked with Harold. Down below, in a kind of hollow, it was very dark; the darkest stretch in the Common. She was always nervous when crossing here, and quickened her pace involuntarily. But her fears were subconscious, tonight; she walked on invisible, billowy clouds, and dreamed wonderful dreams of stardom, of film-star heroes and a film-star husband, of waving, cheering fans, of a triumphal return home to Telham and Hindle Street, and proud, humbled parents—perhaps with Harold Millsom kissing her gently on the cheeks and confessing that he had been wrong.

The faint glow of the green lamps was in the sky, and that was now the only light.

A sound pierced this dream world, and she missed a step.

Then she went on, more quickly, hands tightly clenched, heels digging into the springy turf. She didn't look right or left, but went straight on. She had heard something, hadn't she? Or had it been an owl? People said there was one here. She wouldn't come here alone at night again, it was silly being scared just so as to save an extra twenty minutes' walk the other way round. She simply had to get up to the West End, the bright lights, the theater district; she couldn't bear being at home, hearing her father say that she wouldn't come across a straighter young chap than Harold Millsom if she lived to be a hundred, and her mother calling her a stage-struck little fool whose pretty face would be her ruin.

She heard the sound again.

Someone—panting?

This time, she looked round, a swift, frightened glance. It was very dark, but she could see a pale white shape, not far away: the face of a man or woman.

And whoever it was came hurrying.

Running.

"No," gasped Betty. "No, don't—"

She began to run, too. Her high heels caught in the grass and she stumbled. The unknown pounded after her, much nearer, much louder, panting. She wanted to scream, but no sound would come from her throat. She ran on—on—on.

She reached the top of the second slope. Here the light was better, she could even see the green lamps and the yellow ones of the houses and the shops, she could see the shapes of roofs and the outline of trees. She was safe, or very near safety; she'd just been silly, and needn't have panicked. She need only run comfortably—

Her heel caught in the ground, and she pitched forward.

The fall didn't hurt, but it brought terror back, terror which filled her mind and her body. She tried to scramble to her feet. Now she was panting, too, and the thudding of her heart drowned the sound that the pursuer was making, the pounding unknown creature.

She got to her knees.

A dark shape loomed over her.

"No!" she screamed. "No!"

Great fear welled up in her, terror paralyzed her, even the single word coming from her lips was hoarse and gasping.

"No, no, no!"

Before she could see who it was, she felt hands at her throat, felt fingers biting into her flesh as fingers had bitten into her shoulders earlier. But these hurt more; these were squeezing into her flesh, choking. She kicked and struck and fought with awful desperation, but the agonizing pain stayed at her throat—and it was getting worse. Her lungs were bursting, she couldn't breathe. She felt the burning pressure as the air tried to get out and as she fought to draw more in. But the fingers hurt more and more.

The lights faded, until there was only darkness.

A sharp, knifelike pain shot across Betty's breast. She knew that she was losing consciousness. A strange, pain-wracked darkness filled her head, it was as if someone were filling it with air, hissing and roaring; as if her head and her lungs would burst.

Then her thoughts and the pain she felt and the

fear in her were all gathered together and lost in blackness.

Her assailant bent down, gripped her ankles, and dragged her away from the path, over the grass, toward the silent darkness of the bushes.

2

Chief Inspector West

"Where *is* West?" asked Detective Inspector Turnbull. "Doesn't he ever show up before ten?"

"He was out late last night," a detective sergeant said, tersely.

"What I can't understand is why he always gets the plums," Turnbull complained. "I was told that he had the Old Man in his pocket, now I know it's true. If you keep in with Chatworth you can get away with murder in this place. It wants a bit of cleaning up, if you ask me."

"No one," said the sergeant, coldly, "is asking you."

Turnbull made no further comment, but moved to Roger West's desk, one of five in the large office, and sat down in Roger West's chair. No one in the room told him that this was almost sacrilege. No one in the room would feel in the slightest degree sorry for Turnbull when West told him where to get off. Turnbull, by common consent at Scotland Yard, was riding for a fall. Few who knew him hoped it would be a light one.

10

True, he was a clever swine; if it weren't for his conceit and his low opinion of nearly everyone else, he would be good for the Yard.

Now he sat at West's desk, reading reports from MK Division, Telham, about the murder of a girl named Betty Gelibrand. Funny name, Gelibrand. "Attractive blonde" said the Divisional report—and that would mean another holiday for the Press.

Turnbull read on....

The sergeant went out, and the two Chief Inspectors in the office studiously ignored Turnbull. The telephone on Roger's desk rang.

Turnbull snatched up the receiver.

"Turnbull here.... Oh, good morning, sir...." The change in his tone made both the C.I.s look up, and then glance at each other understandingly. "No, sir, he's not in yet.... I don't think he's in the building, sir.... I will, the moment I can get hold of him, I won't lose a moment."

He rang off.

He looked at the profile of one C.I., a rugged profile; and the broad back of the other.

"That," he announced, "was the great Sir Guy Chatworth himself, and he didn't sound too pleased."

Neither man answered.

Turnbull looked nastily at the profile and the back, then lifted the receiver again. He told the operator to let him know the moment that Chief Inspector West entered the building, before turning back to the report and the scanty oddments of information about Betty Gelibrand. Now and again he sniffed; when he'd finished reading, he took out a packet of Turkish cigarettes and lit one.

"Jim," said one C.I. to the other, after a few minutes, "mind if I open a window?"

"I'll help you," growled the other.

Turnbull pretended to read on.

Two sergeants arrived within three minutes of each other, so there were five men in the office when the door opened and Roger West came in.

West had a way with him wherever he was, whatever he was doing, a kind of restrained briskness, giving an impression that he was anxious to get this particular job over and be tackling the next; yet he could be as patient as Cartwright, the Yard's Job.

Two sergeants and two C.I.s looked up at West and secretly grinned, for they saw the way he glanced at his desk and Turnbull. But Turnbull didn't notice. In spite of the open window, the smell of Turkish tobacco smoke was very strong. There was a look of anticipation among the four: this was where West would tear a strip off a subordinate who used his chair, read reports which were on his desk, and polluted the very air.

West, a broad six feet, dressed in a light-brown suit, with fair curly hair and good features justifying the Yard's nickname of "Handsome," let his blue eyes flicker over the four, and then walked toward Turnbull. His smile of greeting died, he became poker-faced.

He reached the desk, casting a shadow. Turnbull glanced up and started with surprise, even appeared to feel a moment of discomfiture.

"Waiting for me?" asked West.

"Er—yes. Yes, brought this." Turnbull stood up, slowly, and picked up the report. "Job out at Telham. Nineteen-year-old girl murdered. Strangled."

12

The moment of discomfiture past, Turnbull became just a detective with a Yard man's dispassionate attitude toward facts and evidence. "Not a sex job, they say. She scratched the murderer— hands or face. According to the three different descriptions given by three different people out at MK, she was something to look at. A local Beauty Queen."

"Oh," said West.

Turnbull, while talking, had moved out of the way of West's chair. West sat down. The other four, very busy about their own business, all showed disappointment in varying degrees. One could never tell how West would take a thing, but he shouldn't let Turnbull put anything over him; it would make the Detective Inspector even more insufferable.

"Sir Guy wants you to go over to Telham," Turnbull reported; "he's been on the telephone for you several times."

"I've just seen him," West said, briefly. "You're to come on this job with me."

Turnbull's eyes glistened.

"Oh, good. I—"

"It'll be an exercise in logic and deduction, no doubt," West said, "but don't forget that people are involved, will you? Go easy on the parents."

"Oh, to hell with the parents," Turnbull said carelessly. "It's the boy friend I'm interested in, a Harold Millsom."

"Are you?" West looked at him levelly. "I hope he doesn't disappoint you. Telephone MK and say we're on our way. Then go and see if my car's ready, will you? I had a bit of pump trouble on the way here. If the mechanics haven't finished, we'll use anything they can spare. Shouldn't think we'll need anything fast."

"We can use mine," Turnbull offered eagerly. He had a high-powered Jaguar.

"No, thanks," West said.

Turnbull obviously didn't like that, but shrugged and turned away. The door closed behind him. West waved a hand in front of his face, dispersing smoke, glanced at the windows, lit a Virginia cigarette, and then began to look at the reports. He was reading them ten minutes later, when the telephone rang.

"Hallo? ... Yes, Turnbull. ... I'll be right down."

He rang off.

"Handsome," said the Chief Inspector with the rugged profile, "why the hell didn't you tear a strip off him? He wants keeping down, or he'll get unbearable."

"Now could I keep a good man down?" asked West. His smile didn't suggest that he had any kindly feeling toward Turnbull, but that was his only comment. "I'll be seeing you. Urgent messages to MK."

"*O*-kay," the Rugged Profile grinned.

"Tell you what you can do for me," West said, belatedly. "Turn up the files on murdered girls—unsolved jobs—in the past three months or so, will you? Lock 'em away from Mr. Turnbull!"

He went out.

He whistled softly as he walked along the wide, cold passages of the Yard, was taken down in the big lift, and walked down the stone steps into the courtyard. Turnbull was standing by the side of his, West's green Morris.

"Oh, good," said West. "Hop in."

*   *   *

The girl lay upon a stone slab in the cold, dimly lit morgue attached to the MK Divisional Headquarters. Outside, traffic bustled, but the sound hardly disturbed the stillness. The morgue keeper, with the indifference of long experience, switched on a second light over the girl's face.

"See better?" he asked West.

West and Turnbull stared at Betty Gelibrand.

"My," said Turnbull, "someone's going to lose some happy days and nights, she's quite something."

West looked at him sharply; then studied the bruises beneath the girl's chin, some light, some dark, all evidence of the savagery which had been part of the murder. He moved Betty's head and saw where the hair had been torn out, after catching in the bushes as she had been dragged under cover. He looked at the marks of fingers round the neat ankles.

"See that," Turnbull said. "Two or three runs, but no torn threads. Know what that means?"

"What do you think it means?"

"Why, it's as plain as the nose on your face. Smooth hands, office worker—not manual, anyhow." Turnbull was just the machine again. "Probably got the nails trimmed very close, might even be a nail biter. I mean, *you* try grabbing the girl round the ankles." He pushed past West, grabbed, and demonstrated; the body might have been a plaster model. "Difficult to keep your nails off the stockings, and when you pull, you kind of drag so that the nails would almost certainly break the nylon and leave a lot of frayed ends. But they

15

didn't. She's all of ten stone, meaty little filly, but—"

"He could have worn gloves," West said, without any change of expression.

"Gloves and a grip like that?" Turnbull pointed to the bruises on the throat. "You don't think so any more than I do." He sniffed. "It was a warm night, too. Well, not much more we can do here, is there?"

There wasn't.

They spent another half-hour in the office upstairs, looking at photographs, hearing about the girl's parents, her crowning as the Beauty Queen of South London, her hopes and plans, her boy friend Harold Millsom, and a few other odds and ends which the Divisional people thought important and Turnbull obviously didn't. Then they drove to the Common, which was little more than a small park without gates and fences.

It was fresh and green, for there had been a lot of rain that May, and this was early June. The trees were in full leaf. Several clumps of rhododendron glowed pink, purple, and bright red in the warm sun. A crowd surged about the bushes and the nearer trees, and the police had roped off a semi-circle which included the flowering shrubs. Six uniformed policemen stood guard, and a hundred people, several of them women with young children, gaped at the plain-clothes police who were near the lovely flowers which had hidden death.

About all this, the birds sang and flitted; and there was the hum of insects, the unflustered seeking of bees.

West stepped over the rope; Turnbull followed. They saw where the body had been left—where

16

the girl might have stayed for hours, even days, but for a frisky dog and an elderly man who had wondered where the dog had found a handkerchief....

They saw the tracks made when she had been dragged along; and hair was clinging to thorny brambles and small hawthorn bushes.

"If you don't mind me saying so," Turnbull said with ill-concealed impatience, "I think it's time we talked to this boy friend, Millsom. She'd won this Beauty Queen title, small wonder when you think of her face and figure, and she wouldn't have much time for a plodding Harold after that, would she?"

"She might not," West temporized.

Turnbull obviously had to fight to keep calm.

"We don't want the chap to do a flit, do we?"

"Don't we?" For the first time, West's eyes smiled faintly. "Wouldn't that point the accusing finger?"

"You know what I mean," said Turnbull. "The killer's a dangerous type; if it is this Millsom, it would be better to know where he is."

"We'll go and see him, soon," West agreed. "In fact—" He broke off, as one of the policemen at the cordon moved away from a man who had been talking and gesticulating wildly, and came toward him. "Forget it," West added, and went to meet the policeman.

He looked past him toward the man who had been talking and waving his arms about. He was young, and really something to see. A badly swollen mouth, one eye closed up, a cut over the other eye, and a swollen ear, all told their story. Beneath it all was a lean neck and a busy Adam's apple.

The constable saluted.

17

"Excuse me, sir, there's a man here says that he can give you some information."

"Do you know him?"

"Well, I do and I don't," said the constable. "He's a chap named Carter. Tick Carter." The constable didn't actually sneer, but went very close, and so managed to create exactly the impression he wanted to. "He's been around here for years, sir. He says—"

Tick Carter suddenly vaulted over the rope, and hurried toward them at an ungainly gait.

"I tell you I know who it was!" he shouted, as if he were calling through a reed pipe. "It was that swine Millsom! They had a hell of a row here last night. One *hell* of a row, and—and he nearly killed *me*, too. Look at my face. Look—"

"Take it easy, take it easy," boomed the constable, and stemmed the flow of words long enough to give Turnbull a chance to say:

"What did I tell you? I can smell 'em!"

"If I were you, I'd keep my voice down a bit," West said to the gangling Tick Carter. "Now, tell us all about it."

Turnbull already had a notebook and pencil out; his pencil sped, keeping pace with the rush of words, and his face held a look of almost gloating satisfaction.

Ten minutes later, West, Turnbull, and an MK man left for the shop where Millsom worked, in Telham High Street. Ten minutes later still, they discovered that he hadn't shown up that morning.

He had lodgings near by, and his landlady was worried because he hadn't been home all night.

18

3

Second Sight?

"Oh, we'll soon get Mr. Harold Millsom," Turnbull said confidently. "We'll turn on the heat, he won't have a chance." The Detective Inspector grinned at Roger West. "I was pretty sure from the beginning, wasn't I?"

"Second sight?" inquired West, mildly.

"Oh, I wouldn't put it as strong as that," said Turnbull, almost offhandedly, "but you know what it is, don't you? You can almost smell 'em."

He sat next to Roger in the car, grinning. They were in a rush-hour traffic jam, and cars, buses, and lorries were jolting along a few yards at a time, while people on the pavements walked briskly by. The smell of exhaust fumes and of petrol made the warm afternoon unpleasant; and the sun shone down on the massed traffic and walking people. The Yard men were on the inside, because Roger wanted to take the next left turn, and get out of the jam.

Turnbull was an impressive beggar, he reflected —the type who would be a huge success with

19

women. If he weren't so cocksure, he would probably also be a success with men. His hair was auburn, and had a natural wave. He had a fair
complexion, and obviously spent a lot of time sun-
bathing; he had the bronze skin of an addict. He
smiled often, showing big, glistening teeth. There
was some kind of story that he was the son of a
wealthy Australian who had chosen to make a career for himself at the Yard and was heading for
the top as fast as he could go. Roger didn't know
whose son he was and didn't greatly care. He knew
that Turnbull ran the high-powered Jaguar, a
much flashier car than anyone below the rank of
Assistant Commissioner at Scotland Yard could afford.

The bus in front moved slowly.

"*Phweee-oooo!*" Turnbull whistled, and made
Roger look up sharply; and looking, he stalled the
engine.

He started it again, quickly, as he caught a
glimpse of a girl turning the corner—and knew
that Turnbull was looking at her. She meant to be
looked at. She wore a vivid blue cotton dress, a
wide white belt, and a big floppy white hat, and
she carried a huge white bag. She had a figure that
any model would have envied, and knew quite
well that practically every man she passed stared
at her.

"They don't come like that very often," Turnbull
said, turning to watch her go past. "But I bet that
kid could have given her a run for her money."

"What kid?"

"Little Betty Gelibrand."

West bit his tongue, saw the traffic moving, and
slipped through a gap. They didn't speak again

20

until they reached the Yard. Turnbull was humming a tune which Roger didn't know.

Outside the Yard, a newsboy was calling, "Man wanted, paper! Read all abaht the latest murder, paper!" and grinned broadly at the Yard men.

"Insolent swine," Turnbull growled, "I'll clip his ear if he comes it too much."

"Assault is assault," West said, "even if it's by a policeman. Go and write up a report, will you?"

"Can't we do it together?" Turnbull looked affronted.

"No," Roger said shortly. "I'll leave it to you."

Turnbull went off when they reached Roger's floor, in something not far from a huff. Roger smiled bleakly. He went to his office and phoned the Assistant Commissioner, but Chatworth wasn't in. He opened a brown-paper packet he'd brought up, and looked at the photographs: of Betty as she had posed after being crowned the Beauty Queen of South London; of Betty with all the competitors; of Betty with her mother and father. She was an only child. There were also two photographs of Harold Millsom, and several people who knew him swore that each was a good likeness. Judging from that, Millsom was a pleasant-looking man in the late twenties, with a broken nose and untidy hair.

It was dark hair, his friends said; and his eyes were brown, his complexion rather on the swarthy side; well, olive. People seemed to like him; or at least, respect him. He was a leather goods buyer at Telham's one small department store. Roger let his mind roam over the dozens of people they had seen: Millsom's employer, his fellow workers, his juniors; his landlady. The woman had been close on tears.

Then there were the Gelibrands, stricken, shaken, and shaky, the man almost speechless, the woman feverishly garrulous. They'd a lot on their minds. Before Betty had gone out the previous night they'd quarreled—at least, both her mother and father had been sharply critical; if they hadn't been so, she might never have gone out. And if she hadn't gone out . . .

So they reproached themselves with vain bitterness.

Interviewing them, Turnbull had been impatient again. All Turnbull wanted was news of Harold Millsom. He was quick-witted, alert, shrewd, persistent; oh, he was smart. If he made a mistake, it was in assuming that Millsom was the only possible suspect. True, no others had shown up, but it was early yet.

Roger West studied the photographs again.

Betty had been really beautiful; more beautiful than many competition winners, although the one she had won was important. It was run by Conway's, a big soap and soap-powder firm. There were twelve heats, four in London, five others in the rest of England, one each in Scotland, Wales, and Northern Ireland. The finals' winner would really go places.

Yes, the girl had been beautiful enough to make Millsom bitter and angry. Tick Carter—known as Tick since schooldays, Roger now knew, for even then Carter had been regarded as a "nasty little tick"—had been angry too, but truthful. There had been other witnesses, including three youths who had seen Millsom's onslaught on Carter.

Sometimes the easy job came along; sometimes the finger pointed at the only possible suspect.

Turnbull thought it did this time. Roger wasn't convinced, but realized that he might be doubtful simply because Turnbull was so cocksure. He did not like Detective Inspector Turnbull, hoped that he would not have to work with him much, but was determined not to allow his dislike to affect his judgment. Turnbull might be too intense, too dogmatic, and cursed with a single-track mind, but he was good and quick. He'd needed only half a word to get to the telephone and set the Yard moving after Millsom; and he had checked everything in the local hunt for the man swiftly and accurately. The chances were that he was right about Millsom, too.

The door opened. The Rugged Profile came in.

" 'Lo, Handsome, had a nice day?"

"So-so."

"Just seen His Lordship Sir Ruddy Warren Turnbull," said the Rugged Profile. "He's complaining that you're making him write out the report, and afterward you'll sign it and claim that it was all your own work. You ought to jump on him with both feet. I'm going to, the first chance I get."

"Mind you don't hurt your feet," Roger grinned. "Get anything for me?"

"What about?"

"Murdered girls."

"Oh, lor', yes," said the Rugged Profile, and dropped to his chair and rummaged through papers on his desk. "Nine jobs in the past three months, up and down the country. Here you are." He leaned across with a sheaf of reports. "Not that it will tell you much. Three knifed, one drowned, two coshed, three strangled. If there wasn't such a thing as sex," added the Rugged Profile, only half in jest, "it would be a happier world."

"All sex?"

" 'Cept a couple."

Roger read through reports on the cases, sorting them out. Some he remembered, others he'd heard of vaguely. One was very much the same as the murder of Betty Gelibrand, a pretty girl of similar social standard had been strangled; but there had been no apparent motive and only common assault, no violence except the strangling.

He read on.

He began to whistle, beneath his breath.

A carefully prepared sketch of the spot where the body had been found was attached to the report; and it showed a line where the girl's body had been dragged, after death, away from the footpath and behind some bushes. Remove the name, remove the evidence of battered Tick Carter, and forget the disappearance of Harold Millsom, and the two cases could be almost identical. The one Roger was reading about, the murder of a girl named Hilda Shaw, had been at Tottenham, a London district very much like Telham.

The door opened and Turnbull breezed in.

"I've done the report," he said. "Like to read it, or shall I turn it in?"

"I'll look through it," Roger said.

"Thanks, *sir*." Turnbull almost sneered. "Put me right if I've gone wrong. There's a call from Chelsea, they think they've seen Millsom. Okay for me to go and see?"

Roger hesitated, then said, "Yes."

"Oke," said Turnbull, and went out. The door closed with a snap.

24

Roger read the report. It was good; in fact, it was almost brilliant. Turnbull had an easy prose style, which wasn't exactly an accomplishment of many Yard men, he didn't waste words, and he was clever; not far from cunning. Nothing here suggested that he took Millsom's guilt for granted; in fact, he had gone out of his way to recommend that MK Division be asked to speed up inquiries about Betty Gelibrand's other boy friends. "An attractive girl of the type is likely to have many," he had added—his one written mistake, the only time when he had talked down to whoever would read and study the report.

Turnbull had signed it, heavily, in ink.

Smiling faintly, Roger wrote, "Read and approved" and initialed it.

There was Chatworth to see, and developments in a dozen other cases to look at. He was working at too high a pressure; he always was. He ought to be able to leave the Telham job to Turnbull and MK Division, but was teased by the murder of the Tottenham girl. She'd been dragged away by her feet, too, and—

Roger picked up the report again; a factual and thorough one. What about the stockings? Ah—identical, too: "Slight damage to the nylon stockings worn by the deceased."

He rang *Records*.

"Get me everything you can on the murder of Hilda Shaw, at Tottenham, six weeks ago."

"Right away, sir."

"Hold it until I come," Roger said, "don't send it along." He almost surprised himself by saying that, and realized that it was to make sure that

Turnbull didn't find out how his mind was working. He wanted to keep something up his sleeve.

Then Chatworth sent for him—big, burly, grizzle-haired Chatworth, the country farmer in the wrong place, the place being an office of ultra-modern design, black glass and chromium furniture. Chatworth just wanted to be brought up to date. He grumbled, rumbled, and smoked a small cheroot.

"Seems all right, then," he said. "No word from Turnbull about this man Millsom yet?"

"Not yet."

"About Turnbull," Chatworth said. "Is he as good as some people say?"

Roger was ready for that. "He gives me the impression of being very efficient, sir. I don't think you'll find anything wrong with his report."

"Oh," said Chatworth, and rumbled again, and looked thoughtful. "All right, I'll go through it."

Roger went off.

It was nearly six o'clock. He'd had a heavy day, and wanted an evening at home. Why not take one? Janet, his wife, was going through one of her periodic spells of complaint against the Yard, and his having long hours and too much responsibility. An evening at home now would make all the difference to her. He scribbled notes, then reached for his hat—and the telephone bell rang.

He was alone.

He answered, "West speaking....Oh, yes, put him through....Yes, I'll hold on."

He fumbled for cigarettes with his left hand as he held the receiver to his ear. This was Turnbull, who'd persuaded someone to say that he wanted to speak to Chief Inspector West in person—Turnbull

26

being very important and making sure he didn't waste any of his precious time.

He spoke.

"That you, Handsome?" Damn his eyes. "Turnbull here, I think we've got him."

"Millsom?"

"Yep. On the roof of a church, Brickley Street, Chelsea, near Cheyne Walk. Only trouble is, he's got a gun."

Roger said slowly, softly: "Are you sure it's Millsom?"

"I'm going to be surprised if it isn't," said Turnbull. "Thought you ought to know what's on. I'm going up after him."

Roger snapped, "You stay down there. Have the place surrounded and wait for me."

"But—" Turnbull almost howled.

"I said wait!" roared Roger, and banged down the receiver and rushed to the door.

4

The Church

The church rose high above the tall houses near by. Its slender steeple overlooked the broad and gentle Thames, and three bridges and, not far off, the stark grandeur of the Battersea Power Station, which poured thick, dense, white smoke out of a vast chimney and sent it rolling over the roofs of the mean houses on the other side of the river.

Uniformed policemen were controlling a restive crowd. Quiet staff work had brought a black-and-yellow DIVERSION notice, and a hot but placid constable stopped Roger with a sturdy arm raised.

"Sorry, sir, the road's blocked." He had the patient pedantry of London police at times of trial. "If you turn back, take the second on the right, then—"

"I'm West."

"Eh? Who? Oh, Mr. *West*." The barricade of an arm dropped like a railway signal. "Sorry, sir."

Roger drove along the empty section of the street, watched by envious youths, a hundred or more men and women, and a few newspapermen.

He could see the steeple and the metal scaffolding built about the church. He turned a corner, and there was a little group of Divisional police, a fire-fighting unit with the turntable already being extended, firemen in steel helmets—everyone who should be there except Turnbull.

A burly, benevolent-looking man came toward him as he pulled up behind the fire engine. This was the Superintendent of the Division.

"Hallo, Handsome, you didn't lose much time."

" 'Lo, Teddy. Where's my D.I.?"

"Turnbull?"

"Yes."

The Divisional man grimaced.

"Inside. Up on the roof, I shouldn't wonder. There was no holding him."

So Turnbull had defied a specific order. There were moments to be patient, times to be tolerant, but sooner or later with Turnbull, a time to be drastic. This was it. Roger didn't say so to the Divisional man, but nodded, and went toward the open doors of the church. The other walked with him, talking, explaining. There was a way to the roof from the inside as well as from the outside— the steeple was rickety from delayed-action bomb damage, and was now being repaired. The fabric of the church was all right, apart from that and a few holes in the roof. Millsom appeared to have gone there for sanctuary. A passing police constable had seen and recognized him and raised the alarm. There had been one shot, so far—a warning shot fired at the constable inside the church.

"Inside?" Roger asked.

Here, it was gloomy. The side windows were of plain glass, but one colored window beyond the altar was radiant with a glowing beauty, the greater because the evening sun shone upon it, turning to gold a halo upon the picture of Christ.

"Yes," the Divisional man said. "Bullet hit the vestry door. Our chap came in by the vestry. Millsom was climbing up to the roof, then."

They craned their necks.

There were great oak rafters in the roof; more scaffolding; and several places where green canvas awnings gave temporary protection against the weather. The gray stone of the walls made its own peculiar suggestion of massive strength.

Two policemen, helmets off, stood near the chancel steps.

"Not much chance that he'll come back this way," the Divisional man said in a hushed voice. "But I thought we'd better be sure."

"Yes. When did Turnbull come in?"

"Just after 'phoning you."

There was no sign of Turnbull. The two policemen, their voices muted, said that they had seen him disappear behind the altar—it was from there that one could get to the roof from the inside.

"Now that Millsom's outside, this is the safest way up, I suppose," said the Divisional man.

"Yes," agreed Roger. No one else moved, there was no sound but their breathing. He called, "Turnbull." He didn't shout, but his voice was loud, and the sound echoed about the cool, quiet building. "Turnbull!"

A man appeared from the vestry.

It may have been a trick of the light, but for a moment he did not look like a man of the flesh, rather one apart from this world. That was partly because of his pale face, partly because of his ex-

pression, one of strange serenity—a kind of serenity which looked as if it would not last long, being
imposed upon him rather than springing from
great inner strength.

He was dressed in clerical gray, and wore a clerical collar.

Roger thought, "Where have I seen him before?"

The clergyman came forward.

"I know you must make some noise," he said
quietly. "I'm not used to shouting in here."

"No," Roger said. "Sorry. Did you see Millsom?"

The man's eyes closed for a moment, as if he
were hurt, or as if light dazzled him. Then he
looked Roger full in the eyes.

"No," he said.

Something in his manner made Roger doubtful,
but he didn't ponder over that.

"Pity," he said. "Have you seen anyone else?"

"I've seen several policemen, including the man
who went up to the roof."

"So he's up there, is he?" Roger said grimly.

He touched the gun in his pocket. He didn't like
carrying a gun, but when a wanted man was
known to be armed, it was folly not to have one.
He didn't like the idea of a gun fight in or on top of
a church, either, but there was the mark of a bullet
on the dark, age-worn oak of the vestry door.

"I'll go up after him," Roger said to the Divisional man. "We won't be any more of a nuisance
than we can help, sir."

He nodded to the clergyman, and turned away,
wondering why the man had raised his doubts
with that emphatic "no," wondering now if a parson could have lied when standing so close to the
altar steps and the communion rail. Then Roger

31

forgot the parson, the Divisional man, everyone else. He started to climb up the scaffolding. It was easy to see where Turnbull had gone. You had to concede the man courage; he wasn't armed, but knew that Millsom was.

Roger climbed higher and higher.

Looking down, the nave, the pews, the glistening brass eagle at the lectern, the carved choir stalls, the altar and the lovely flowers on it, all looked small; miniature; so did the policemen and the parson.

"I've seen him before," Roger thought again, and then stared up.

Light came through a hole in the roof, where the canvas covered it. He pushed the canvas aside. It was easy to climb out from here, and the bright light of the sunlit evening hurt his eyes.

Not far along was the base of the steeple, about it a forest of steel scaffolding. There was no sign of Millsom or Turnbull, but Roger couldn't see far because of a little wooden hut, perched on the scaffolding like a giant crow's nest. Between this and Roger was a wide gap in the scaffolding, bridged by two narrow planks of wood.

To the right and the left were the gray roofs of houses; ahead, the broad strip of the Thames burnished by the sun. There was also the power station pouring out its mass of smoke.

"Turnbull!" Roger called.

There was no answer.

"Turnbull!"

There came a creaking sound; then Turnbull's head appeared at the open doorway of the little hut. The sun made his hair look as if it was of burnished copper. His eyes glistened, and he looked viciously angry.

"Why the hell can't you keep quiet? He—" Turnbull broke off abruptly, obviously hadn't realized that the caller was Roger. There was a moment's pause; then, "Sorry." His voice was just a whisper. "Think I've cornered him."

This wasn't the time to tell Turnbull where to get off.

"Where?"

"Other side of this tool shed," said Turnbull, still whispering. "I'm trying to prize some boards out, to get at him. I'm afraid he'll jump off if we're not careful. Rather see him hanged than break his neck the other way! Leave this to me, will you?"

"No. I'm coming across."

"Listen," Turnbull protested, "I'm here, I can manage. It's dangerous and—"

"Stand by," Roger said.

Turnbull looked at him angrily, but didn't protest again. It was dangerous all right; just the two planks across a ten-foot gap and a drop to sun-baked ground and gravestones covered with lichen, softly green. A drop to death. Millsom lurked somewhere behind Turnbull and the shed, and Roger wanted Millsom alive, but wasn't sure that Turnbull was the right one to get him. Turnbull wouldn't reason with the wanted man.

Roger stepped onto the planks.

He stretched his arms out on either side, to keep his balance. It was only ten feet away, but looked much farther. Turnbull was glaring, but stretching out a hand to give support the moment Roger reached the other side. There was really nothing to it.

33

He was halfway over. then, *cra-ack*, came the shot.

Roger heard it, thought he saw a tiny flash, felt a biting pain at his leg. He staggered. His heart made one convulsive leap, as if it had turned right over. The grass, the gravestones, the headstones, the men, the guttering and the granite sides of the church were all below him, he was falling toward them, he hadn't a chance.

He grabbed at a piece of steel scaffolding, and clutched it. As it stopped him, his arms seemed wrenched out of their sockets. He groaned as he hung full length, a hundred and fifty feet from the ground, with pain tearing at his shoulders.

He couldn't hold on for long, his right hand was already slipping. He felt it going. His only chance of getting firm hold with both hands was to lift his right and grab again.

He took the chance.

He grabbed and missed.

The pain at his left shoulder became far greater. He couldn't get his foot against the wall or against any piece of scaffolding. He was quite sure that he was going to fall, and that in falling he would smash himself to death. He could think quite calmly of Janet and his two sons; as if they were physically near him. He could imagine his wife's voice vividly. That was all—except for the increasing pain at his shoulder because all of his fourteen stone were on it; and a gradual movement of the palm of his hand and his fingers as they slid round the piece of rounded steel.

He couldn't hold on for more than two or three minutes, and there was no chance of help from below. Just death, waiting to catch him.

"*West*," called Turnbull, in a piercing voice.

Roger moved his head, slowly, painfully; he dared not do anything in a hurry.

"Listen," Turnbull called. He was above Roger, kneeling by the little hut. "Listen, I'm coming. Hold on, I'm coming."

He'd kill himself.

"No! Don't—"

"Just hold on, you bloody fool!"

Millsom, who could see them although he wasn't in sight, would probably shoot again.

"Go back!"

"Hold on," Turnbull called.

He was edging toward the piece of scaffolding, along the planks. He dared not move too quickly for fear of losing his balance. Now he was on one knee, kneeling on the planks across which Roger had walked. If Millsom fired, Turnbull would make the easiest target anyone could wish for.

Roger's hand was slipping; slowly, remorselessly.

"Hold on, West."

"You'll fall, go back."

"Come on," Turnbull said. "Lend a hand."

He lowered himself with painful slowness, until he lay full length on his stomach, his body overlapping the boards on either side. His long right arm stretched downward, the hand crooked, to grip. He didn't need to speak; he wanted Roger to raise his right hand, so that they could grip each other, and then he might be able to support Roger long enough for the fire turntable to come, or for help with ropes.

On the other hand, he might overbalance.

Or Millsom might shoot him.

"Come—on," Turnbull breathed, hoarsely.

Roger raised his right arm. It wasn't easy because the movement of his body thrust greater weight on his left shoulder, and pain tore at him. He gritted his teeth and closed his eyes, but managed to raise his right hand. He felt the touch of Turnbull's fingers—hard and firm. Then came the grip of the other man's hand, and some of the weight was eased from his shoulder.

"Now we won't be long," Turnbull said. "Take it easy."

His left arm was underneath the boards, holding on, and his grip was powerful and steady. But Roger could see the sweat beading his forehead and gathering in his eyes. There were other things to make him think, too. Voices below, noises as if an engine were starting up, men shouting as if calling orders.

The firemen were bringing an escape ladder. Roger had a distorted view of them crossing the churchyard at the double.

Where was Millsom? Why had he fired before if he wasn't going to fire again? Why—

Somewhere near by but not just below, a man or woman screamed.

The scream went through Roger like an electric shock. He flinched, felt Turnbull react the same way, swayed—and then heard a different sound; a thud. Hanging there, it seemed as if he was hearing the sound of his own body hitting the ground.

The scream came again.

5

The Father

Turnbull did not flinch at the second scream, but was very tense and rigid, while Roger waited fearfully for a third. It did not come; instead there was an outburst of sobbing, and gradually words themselves floated on the soft evening air.

"He's dead, look, he's dead."

Men spoke; the voices quietened; it was as if a soothing murmur rose from the spot which was out of sight. Some men working to get the ladders into position made much more noise, yet it did not drown the other.

Soon the firemen came hurrying up, nimble, seeming careless to the novitiate. They talked quietly, expertly, deftly, telling Roger and Turnbull exactly what to do. It seemed a long time, but it wasn't so long before Roger was safely on firm scaffolding.

Turnbull was arguing.

"Take him first," he said to the firemen. "I'm all right. Just look at him, out on his feet, white as a sheet."

They let him have his way.

Roger was slung over a man's shoulder. He had to clench his teeth because his own shoulder hurt so much. His left leg did, too. Something wet and warm was running down it; when he put his foot on the ground, he seemed to be treading in a sticky pool.

"Steady," a man said.

"Lay him down," said another, authoritatively. "Let's have a look at that leg."

"Bleeding like a pig," contributed a third.

They helped Roger to sit on the ground, and he couldn't keep back a gasp when someone jolted his shoulder.

"What, more trouble?" said the man with the authoritative voice.

"I'm—all right. What—happened round there?"

"Don't know and couldn't care less," said the fireman. "Easy, now—"

It wasn't long before a doctor arrived; then an ambulance; and soon they put Roger on a stretcher, with the wound in his leg padded to stop the bleeding, and his shoulder thick with a temporary strapping. The pain came like waves of the sea, smashing at him ceaselessly; pain which nothing seemed to stop.

Turnbull looked aggressively healthy as he stood staring down at the stretcher.

"Bad luck, Handsome, but it'll give you a couple of weeks' sick leave." He grinned, as if rejoicing. "I'll tell your missus, don't worry."

"What happened—"

"Millsom threw himself over," said Turnbull. "He's just a nasty mess on the pavement. Couldn't be helped, I suppose."

He wouldn't say that to others; he would say that Millsom would have been taken alive if Roger West hadn't thrown his weight about. That was as nearly certain as anything could be.

"Oh," Roger grunted. "My fault. Er—"

"Oh, forget it!"

"Not so easy," Roger said, and twisted his lips against another wave of pain. He felt the sweat running down his forehead in tiny beads. "Thanks for what—you did—up there."

Turnbull grinned almost fiercely.

"Forget that, too. Hi, Doc!" Someone had come round the corner of the church. "Got a shot of morphia? The boss needs one."

The doctor was the Divisional police surgeon, gray, grave, well-prepared. He busied himself; an ambulance man bared Roger's arm, the needle plunged in, and more agonizing pain stabbed at the shoulder.

"Be gentle with him," the doctor cautioned.

Two men lifted the stretcher, and no one could be blamed for the pain Roger felt. He ought to sing about it, for he was alive when he might so easily have been dead. He saw the scaffolding against the sky, and the plank off which he had slipped; it hurt even to think of hanging by one hand from that iron tubing. If it hadn't been for Turnbull's cold, calm courage, there would be another mess on the ground.

They went out of the churchyard.

Police had cordoned off a spot. Turnbull, going ahead of Roger, reached it first. Roger could see only from a distance of twenty yards or more. There was a woman being carried away, and the parson on his knees by the side of something which was covered with a piece of the green canvas used for the work on the church. The parson's face was bowed, but even in that position he was vaguely familiar; irritatingly familiar.

The pain wasn't so bad, now. Roger felt drowsy with a different kind of wave sweeping over him; these were gentle waves. But he was a long way from unconscious. He was even beginning to wonder why Millsom had fired at him, Roger West, and not troubled to shoot at Turnbull. Had he been terrified, fired almost without thinking, and afterward realized that nothing he could do would help him?

He'd been a long time deciding to jump off.

Turnbull's voice startled Roger.

"We can't stay here all day, even for you." He was harsh, almost brutal, as he spoke to the clergyman. "Nothing more you can do for him, anyhow. You missed your chance while he was alive."

The clergyman's face, pale and grave until then, became the face of a different being. Such pain suffused it that even Turnbull was shocked into brief silence. One of the ambulance men must have been looking; involuntarily he allowed his end of the stretcher to drop a few inches. Roger could see nothing but the pale face and the torment possessing it. He was ten yards away; he saw the picture as he could have seen a film close-up.

"Ever seen him before?" Turnbull demanded.

There was a long, long pause; and then the clergyman's face lost a little of the agony, and he answered very quietly.

"Yes," he said, "he was my son."

So he was Millsom's father; no wonder there was a likeness! And he was racked by his grief and distress and perhaps remorse.

What did Turnbull think? What went on in his mind now that he knew he had spoken so brutally to the dead man's father, half-jeering while saying, "You missed your chance while he was alive." What did Millsom's father think?

The new waves, the quiet, peaceful waves, were now coming very fast.

Roger lost consciousness.

Martin West, often called Scoopy, was walking along Bell Street, Chelsea, when he saw his father's car turn into the street, and his eyes lit up. He was carrying his precious cricket bat and a pair of pads fastened to it by the straps. He hoisted these to his sturdy shoulder as he broke into a run.

He passed the open garden gate of his house, where his brother, Richard, was watching a bird's nest high in a tree.

"Dad's coming!" cried Martin.

"Oh, good!" called Richard, a tall, slender nine. He left the birds to look after themselves, and raced into the street. "Ask him for a ride!" he shouted to Martin.

At the bedroom window Janet West heard and saw them both. She had been about to call them in; they ought to have been getting ready for bed, but it was a glorious June evening, and she hadn't had the heart to make them come earlier. She watched them running, and then frowned, for Roger did not slow down. Usually he spotted the boys in a moment, and would stop for them to clamber in—sometimes teasing for a few moments by pretending that the brakes wouldn't hold.

Ten-year-old Martin first, then Richard, stood and gaped as the car flashed by them.

It was going much too fast, too.

"What on earth's the matter with Roger?" Janet asked aloud, and stared out.

Tires squealed as the car jolted, and then came to a standstill outside the house. Roger wasn't going to put it in the garage, he must be in a tearing hurry. That explained much, but not the way he had passed the boys. He didn't usually drive so fast, even when he was rushed. He—

A stranger climbed out.

But it was Roger's car, wasn't it?

The boys, hurrying, were now side by side, and watching the stranger with as much curiosity as Janet.

The man was something to see. He was taller than Roger, and quite remarkable. Janet found herself smiling down at him. He walked briskly toward the front door. His hair was auburn and ridiculously curly, the kind of hair a woman would give a fortune for. He went out of sight onto the porch; and knocked and rang.

The boys reached the gate.

Janet moved suddenly, and ran across the room, seized by a sudden panic. What on earth was she thinking of? Who would come in Roger's car except a policeman bringing bad news? Could it be trouble? Surely someone would have telephoned ...no, the Yard preferred to send a messenger at such times, but would they send a stranger?

She flew to the front door, and opened it.

"So you're Handsome's young feller-me-lads, are you?" the stranger was saying. He had his back to the door, and apparently didn't hear it open. "Wouldn't have any doubt that he was *your* father," he added, and ruffled Martin's hair. The elder boy ducked and backed away. Janet saw the stranger's profile, and the way he grinned as he tweaked one of Richard's large, outstanding ears. "Wouldn't like to be so sure about you! Is your mother in?"

"Yes, sir," said Martin, from a distance. "But please, is there anything the matter with my father?"

"Plenty, Sonny Jim," said the stranger, but his grin belied the words. Janet now believed that he knew she was there, and was deliberately keeping her waiting. "He's going to have a few days in hospital and then a week or so's sick leave. He's hurt his arm."

"Arm!" exclaimed Janet, and moved forward. "Is that all? Are you sure?"

She clutched the stranger's sleeve.

He turned to look at her, opened his mouth to speak, but didn't utter a word. He just stared, while the boys watched him closely and with sharp interest. The admiration which showed in his eyes was plain enough to Janet, but meant nothing to the boys. Nor did the way the stranger freed his sleeve, took her hand, and squeezed.

"Sure I'm sure, Mrs. West," he said, and broke the spell with a deep laugh; a bronzed Apollo. "I saw him into the ambulance myself—dislocated shoulder and a few pulled muscles, I'd say, and a flesh wound in the leg. Nothing he won't be laughing about soon. And the nasty piece of work who was responsible won't cause any more damage to man or beast." He winked; as if to tell Janet that she could understand what he meant, but the boys mustn't. "I promised him I'd come and tell you myself. I'm Warren Turnbull—Detective Inspector, C.I.D." He gave a mock salute and a dazzling smile, and the admiration was still brazen in his brown eyes.

Richard broke into a delighted giggling laugh; in spite of the tweaked ear, he had been won over. Martin was sober-faced and still kept his distance.

"It—it's very good of you to come," Janet said. "And if he's no worse—"

"My word on it. He's at St. George's Hospital now, and nothing at all to worry about."

"That's a relief," said Janet, and then added hurriedly: "I must telephone, and—but I shouldn't keep you on the doorstep. Won't you come in?"

She hoped he would say that he was sorry he couldn't stay; but she didn't think he would. She was right, too. She took him into the front room, and asked him to sit down, mechanically, picked up the telephone directory, and found the hospital number.

Turnbull grinned, as if amused at her anxiety and determination to do this herself.

The hospital report was fairly reassuring. Janet decided to go there as soon as Turnbull had gone, she had to make absolutely sure. Now the least she could do was to offer him a drink.

"Do sit down," she said.

He sat in Roger's rather worn hide armchair, with his back to the window.

The boys had followed them in, and hovered in the doorway.

"What can I get you?" Janet asked.

44

"Oh, anything, Mrs. West—from whisky to beer! Ever seen anything like this, chaps?" Turnbull leaned forward and tweaked Richard's ear again; two pennies clinked in his hand. "Well, well, well, what a son for a copper, coining money under my very eyes! What about you?" He shot out a hand and touched Martin's nose before the older boy could back away. Pennies clinked.

"Ooh, that's wonderful!" exclaimed Richard. "Do it again."

"Take my advice, young 'un, and never do the same trick twice," advised Turnbull. "Always have something fresh up your sleeve." He winked at Janet again, then took a pingpong ball from his mouth. "See what I mean?"

"It's *marv*elous," cried Richard.

Janet mixed a whisky and soda...

Three quarters of an hour later she managed to get the boys upstairs to start getting ready for bed. They were dazed with a succession of sleight-of-hand tricks which were all clever and quick. Turnbull had a lively patter, and found plenty of time to drink two whiskies, and several opportunities to wink at Janet. He had a curious effect on her. His open admiration had something naïvely boyish about it, but he wasn't naïve or a boy. His wink carried an unmistakable innuendo, if she cared to see it. Now and again he gripped her arm or squeezed her hand, always in the course of performing a trick—but never strictly necessary. He made her feel a little uneasy, but he was a magnificent-looking man, and even made Roger seem small. Well, not exactly small...

She hoped he wouldn't linger when the boys had gone upstairs.

He was standing by the side of his chair, smiling but brisk.

"I must be on my way—regretfully," he said. "I don't mind telling you that I envy Handsome!" His eyes laughed at her, saying she could make what she liked of that. "Two promising kiddos, too," he went on. "I'd like to take 'em out for a day sometime. We'd have fun." He put out a hand. "*Au revoir*, Mrs. West."

He shook hands without squeezing.

He walked away, forgetting to offer to put the car into the garage.

Janet had to make herself back away from the door, and avoid watching him until he was out of sight. She'd never met anyone quite like Turnbull. He had almost succeeded in making her feel sure that Roger wasn't badly hurt, too.

She rang Scotland Yard and was soon speaking to the Rugged Profile.

"Lord, yes, he'll be as right as rain in a few days," the Chief Inspector said. "But mind you, he was lucky. Young Turnbull saved his life, risking his own into the bargain. If Turnbull has any sense, he can make himself the best-liked man at the Yard, now—bar Roger."

"You mean—Detective Inspector Turnbull saved him?" Janet exclaimed.

"That's the chap," the C.I. said. "Why so surprised?"

"He came and told me what had happened to Roger, but didn't say anything about his part in it."

The C.I. made startled noises. Then: "...if Turnbull can be a modest hero I'll believe in miracles," he said. "Anyway, you needn't worry about Roger."

When she rang off, Janet was quite convinced that there was nothing seriously the matter with Roger. Yet she wasn't quite at ease. It wasn't fear or anxiety or even anger that Roger should be exposed to danger again. It was something she didn't quite understand.

That night, when Roger was still under morphia, Turnbull was having fun at a little-known night spot, Millsom's father was sitting in his study, staring at a cross, and Janet and the boys were asleep, another girl was murdered.

This time, the body was dragged behind bushes which were not likely to be disturbed for days; or even weeks.

6

Two Weeks Later

"You all right now, Handsome?"

"Fine, thanks."

"Better, Handsome?"

"Yes, thanks."

"Still limping a bit, aren't you, Handsome?"

"Habit, that's all."

"Glad to see you back, sir."

"Thanks, Simpson."

It was like running a gauntlet, from the gates of the Yard, up the steps through pelting rain, into the damp hallway, up the lift, along the wide green passage and the doors which seemed to open by remote control to allow a face to appear and the inevitable question to come.

Roger reached his own office.

It was nearly nine o'clock on the fifteenth day after his visit to the Chelsea church of St. Cleo's. Outside, black clouds opened to let rain spill out. It hurtled onto the Embankment, pelted through the vivid green foliage of the plane trees outside the window, smashed against the glass, churned up the Thames. No one else was in the office, and Roger stood and looked at the river and remembered how it had seemed when bathed in sunlight just before he had been shot.

The door opened, and Eddie Day came in. He was the Yard's genius on forgery of all kinds, a big man with a huge belly, a receding forehead and receding chin, and prominent teeth which were choked with stoppings.

"Why, 'allo, 'Andsome. Back again? Sure you're well enough?"

"I'm fine, Eddie, thanks," Roger said mechanically.

"Must say we've missed you," conceded Eddie Day. " 'Eard—*heard* all the news?" He rattled off several items. "Coroner sewed everything up for the Gelibrand job, practically told the jury to say it was murder at the hand of Harold Millsom. Lumme," went on Eddie, "Turnbull's hands must be fair worn out!"

Roger's eyes flickered with keener interest.

"What do you mean?"

"The way he's rubbed 'em with satisfaction. And all the time he looked as if he was saying 'I told you so.' But I 'and—*hand*—it to 'im, 'Andsome, he hasn't crowed. Well, not much. Quietened him down a bit, too. Mind you, he's still the best detective at li'l ole Scotland Yard, but he doesn't say so the same nasty way. You've made him almost popular!"

Eddie often talked like a fool and looked like a fool, but in fact he was shrewd; and just now, probing.

"Well, I owe him plenty," Roger said.

"That's the thing that's done him more good

than anything else," said Eddie. "He didn't tell anyone what he did, just waited for others to tell it."

"You haven't a mean and uncharitable spirit, Eddie, have you?"

"Just between you and me," Eddie Day said earnestly, "I don't like Warren Turnbull now any more than I did before, but there's no doubt he's getting round a lot of people. I don't quite know what he's up to, but it's something. P'raps it's just cashing in on prestige." Eddie's lips curled. "Still, you've got to hand it to 'im, 'Andsome, 'e was right there with Millsom, from the word go. Funny chap. Uncanny, in a way; he's done that several times now."

"Done what?"

"Put a finger on the murderer from the word go and been right," explained Eddie, and then the telephone on his desk rang.

He swiveled round to answer it, and Roger sat at his desk. It wasn't piled up with papers, for other Chief Inspectors had taken over most of his work. There were several reports on cases which had been cleared up, others on arrests made and charges pending. All was familiar routine. Crime was like the weather, there was always some kind of it.

There was also a thick file on the Gelibrand case, with full reports of the Coroner's inquest on both pretty Betty and Harold Millsom. Roger read these closely.

Then there was a note from *Records*, too. "Still holding that stuff on Hilda Shaw."

Roger went along to the *Records* office, throwing "Fine, thanks," right and left as he walked. The morning should see this manifestation of good will over.

He found the Inspector in Charge out, but Hilda Shaw's *dossier* was waiting. He took it back to his office, and read it through. Everything was identical with Betty Gelibrand's murder, and there was one totally unexpected thing. She had won a Beauty Competition only a few weeks before her death, but the competition was not specified; a piece of bad reporting. He must check. At half-past ten, Chatworth sent for him.

"Glad to see you back," Chatworth said, looking up from his desk as Roger entered. "All right now?.... Good! Don't overdo it, the first few days. Now, about Turnbull—sit down, man, sit down!— did he go up to that roof against your orders?"

Chatworth had a genius for slinging the unexpected question; Roger a genius for dealing with him.

He smiled amiably.

"He was on the spot and in charge, and had to make the decision. It's a good job for me he was up there."

"If he hadn't been it might never have happened," Chatworth remarked dryly. "Roger, all in confidence, of course—is he good enough for promotion yet?"

"He's very good indeed."

"*But* what?"

"I haven't worked with him very often, sir. What I've seen is first rate. He's a bit impetuous, perhaps, but he knows his own mind and isn't afraid to back himself."

"I'm asking whether he's good enough." Chatworth became gruff.

Roger smoothed down his corn-colored hair. He wished the question hadn't been forced, but there was no evading it now. Still, he waited. Outside, the rain still smashed at the window, and a desk light was on at Chatworth's desk.

"I should say that Turnbull is very good indeed, sir, with more experience he'll probably be brilliant. I'd rather like to see ..." He paused.

Chatworth rumbled, "Go on, go on."

"I'd like to see what he'd do if a couple of cases went sour on him," Roger finished. "I'd be able to judge better if I saw how he reacted."

"H'm, that's a thought. Thanks. Had time to go through the Gelibrand business?"

"Yes, sir."

"Satisfied?"

"No."

Chatworth was so surprised that he sat up abruptly, and light from the top of the lamp shone just beneath his chin, making strange shadows of his face.

"Why the blazes not?"

"There was another job ..." Roger talked, briefly, quietly, and knew that Chatworth was listening intently.

As he described the position in which Hilda Shaw's body had been found and showed the similarities between the two murders, his earlier doubts were strengthened. Chatworth was impressed, too. He forgot to light his cheroot when it went out; and he pondered for several minutes before making any comment. Then:

"I see what you mean. And if the same man killed Hilda Shaw and Betty Gelibrand, both

52

Beauty Queens, we can't assume it was Harold Millsom."

"Not until we've made sure whether Millsom knew Hilda Shaw, knew the Tottenham district, all that kind of thing," Roger said. "I'd like to talk to the Division over there and make a few discreet inquiries."

"You mean, without telling Turnbull?"

"Without telling anyone."

"All right, go ahead," said Chatworth. "I've made some plans for you, and this will fit in nicely. I'd like you to check our liaison with the Divisions, make sure that all of them are happy about the way we're dealing with them!" He gave a quick smile, startlingly sunny, and his face became astonishingly like a baby's for a few seconds. "I like to keep everyone happy, and this will give you a few days to acclimatize yourself."

"Fine," said Roger, and meant it. "Thanks, sir."

"Let's know how things go," said Chatworth.

Roger went out, feeling happier; at least he could give himself his head, and during the coming week he should get some idea whether he was justified in thinking that the two murders had been committed by the same man, and if that man was Millsom. If it wasn't, if the killer of two girls was still loose, there were going to be breakers ahead. It was possible to feel almost sure that Millsom had killed Betty Gelibrand—if he hadn't, why had he run away, and why had he killed himself?

No guess was wholly satisfying.

Roger decided to get someone at MK to find out if Harold Millsom had any association with Tottenham. They'd keep it quiet if he asked them to.

Then he would see Millsom's father.

He was about to leave for Chelsea and the church when the office door opened and Turnbull came in. Until that moment, the office had been just a room with five desks, lights over three of them, and rain still tapping at the window but without the venom of earlier morning. Now, all that changed. Turnbull strode in, affecting everyone there; each man turned to glance at him. He was a disturbing influence, and knew exactly how to make an entrance.

He saw Roger, and his eyes lit up.

"Why, hallo, Handsome, damned glad you're back!" He came striding over, hand outstretched; he had a powerful grip. "At least you've a pretty clear desk, crime's been on the down-and-down for the past fortnight!" He grinned. "That won't last. Satisfied about Millsom?"

"Ugly business altogether," Roger said.

"Only pity was we didn't have him to hang," said Turnbull. "Well, happy convalescence! I want a word with our so-called forgery expert!" He swung across to Eddie Day, magnificently free of movement; a leopard of a man.

Roger looked at his broad shoulders and burnished head, then rubbed his chin and went out.

The Reverend Charles Millsom, Vicar of St. Cleo's, was standing by French windows which opened onto a small, neat lawn, a brick-walled garden with one herbaceous border still bright and colorful although the rain had beaten down the taller flowers and small shrubs, and made the leaves glisten. Now the sun was breaking through the heavy clouds, and shone on the vicar's graying hair, his pleasant face. Much of the hurt had healed, or else he had buried it deep inside him, so that no one else could see.

"Good morning, Chief Inspector." They shook hands. "I hoped that everything was finished."

Roger said, "Did you?" in a way which made the other man's eyes narrow questioningly. "All over and forgotten, is that the way you want it?"

Millsom said slowly, "I don't quite understand you. It's better forgotten. Nothing I can say can move Scotland Yard or coroners, can it? I am quite sure that my son did not kill the girl, but what else is there for me to do?"

Roger moved to the window.

"May I smoke?" He lit up when Millsom refused a cigarette. "Not my job to try to teach you your business," he said, "but what does 'quite sure' mean? A hunch? Blind faith? Or have you any evidence?"

Millsom was standing very still, dressed in the gray suit that was almost black, and the sheer white collar; in his pale face the eyes had suddenly begun to spark.

"What is in your mind, Chief Inspector?"

"There's always the same thing in my mind," Roger said. "A need for facts—a thirst for facts. At Scotland Yard we live by them, can build cases on them, can hang men on them. It might interest you to know we can also prove innocence by them, and that gives most of us a lot more pleasure than proving guilt. Like all of us at the Yard, I'm interested in getting justice for the living and the dead —if they come within my orbit." He had hardly touched his cigarette. "Do you know that your son

55

didn't kill Betty Gelibrand, or are you just guessing and being sentimental?"

He felt that he was almost as brutal as Turnbull. He believed that his tactics were right.

"I'm not absolutely sure," Millsom answered very slowly, "but I think I can offer you some evidence that he didn't kill her." His voice was so low that Roger hardly heard the words. "I talked to —to the other Inspector, Turnbull. I didn't dream from what he said that anyone would listen to me."

"Didn't you?" said Roger; he could picture Turnbull's sneering face. "What's the evidence, Mr. Millsom?"

"I think my son was here at the time that the girl died," Millsom said.

7

More Beauty

Roger left St. Cleo's, an hour later, with plenty more to think about. Millsom had no evidence that his son had been in the vicarage at the time of the murder; but Harold Millsom had called to see him that night, had been very distressed, talked of leaving the country, and even, in a wild moment, of killing himself.

It wasn't until after the inquest that Millsom had realized that he could offer something approaching an alibi for his son. After the disheartening interview with Turnbull, he had made no further effort, believing it would be fruitless, and perhaps do more harm than good, in spite of the facts.

Harold Millsom had been waiting at the vicarage when his father had returned from a parochial meeting, a little after eleven o'clock on the night of the murder. Harold hadn't said what time he had arrived, and had let himself in with a key which he'd taken from under a stone—knowing that for years a key had been left there. No one else had been at the vicarage that evening.

"Just what was his manner like?" Roger had asked.

"He was very agitated indeed," the clergyman had replied quietly. "Obviously in great distress of mind."

"Did he talk about Betty Gelibrand?"

"No."

"Did he give you any idea why he was so distressed?"

"I gathered it was a love affair which had gone badly wrong."

"And you put his behavior down to a kind of hysteria because of his disappointment?"

"Yes."

"How long did he stay?"

"He went up to his room. I expected him to stay the night. The bed was slept in, but he was gone before daybreak. I didn't see him again," the clergyman had added very quietly.

Roger hadn't questioned him much more.

Now Roger drove to the Chelsea Divisional H.Q., and saw the benevolent-looking Superintendent who had led him into the church. He was a gray-haired man with a quiff, a big jowl, and a very florid complexion; a jolly sailor of a man.

He was brisk and amiable, too.

"Yes, Teddy, I'm better, I can walk, and my shoulder will stand any normal strain, thanks very much!" Roger greeted.

"You haven't changed, either. What's this, a ceremonial visit? I'm told that Chatworth wants a lion and a lamb job—hopes to improve Yard and Divisional good will."

Roger chuckled.

"He doesn't know what a hopeless job he's got with the Divisions. Stubborn lot of no-good know-alls."

"You wouldn't be mixing us up with Turnbull, would you?"

"Let's forget it," Roger surrendered. "Teddy, will you find out if a man was seen to enter St. Cleo's vicarage the night before young Millsom died? Somewhere between seven o'clock and eleven."

"What's this? Not satisfied?" The Divisional man was first surprised, then obviously skeptical. "I don't think—"

"Just checking," Roger said. "Will you fix it?"

"Oh, all right."

"Keep it quiet, too. What happened up on the roof of St. Cleo's after the fuss had died down, by the way? Turnbull's report covers everything except that."

"Wasn't much left to happen, was there?" asked the Divisional man. "Turnbull and I went up and had a look round. Then my chaps took some pictures. I can't say there was much to see. Millsom took the gun with him, the only thing that ever puzzled me was why he took a potshot at you and then threw his hand in. If he was in a killing mood you'd think it would last longer than that, wouldn't you?"

"Much longer. No one saw him jump, according to the report, but presumably you saw the spot he jumped from?"

"Well, yes—more or less. Photographed it too. Handsome, what's on your mind?"

"Did you go through the roof, inside and outside,

to check everything and make sure that Millsom was alone?"

The Divisional man just didn't answer. He was standing by his cluttered desk, then suddenly dropped into a chair as if his legs wouldn't support him any longer. He groped for his pipe, obviously seeking some solace.

"I don't think I ever did like you," he growled.

"No, we didn't. Come to think, we were damned casual about it. But I didn't even give a thought to the possibility—oh, go jump on yourself! You're fooling."

"Cross my heart, I mean it," Roger grinned. "Mind if I look at the photographs?" The other man handed over a set, and Roger sat on a corner of the desk looking at them. Outside the sun shone brightly now, and traffic was far enough away for its noise not to matter. "Did you hear the gun hit the ground?"

"Er—no."

"It was lying on the grass, wasn't it?"

"So no one would hear it—the thud of the body would drown the sound, anyhow," argued the Divisional man.

Roger said, "Look," and held out two photographs. There were X's to mark the spots; outlines of gravestones, of the grass of the churchyard, of the pavement—everything visible from the scaffolding; the usual routine had been done. "Body on the actual path, there, gun on the grass five or six yards away. Yards, mind you. If he had the gun in his hand when he jumped the gun would probably drop somewhere between the spot where he fell and the wall of the church. He'd let go of the gun, wouldn't throw it, would he? According to this it's a long way off, nearer the gate. Don't say it could have bounced—there's the indention of the spot where it hit the grass, and it wouldn't have made such a mark if it hadn't fallen from a height. If we're to believe that evidence, Millsom threw the gun first, then jumped. Think so?"

"Why—why should he?"

"That's what's worrying me. Now look at these," Roger said. They were close-up photographs of the steel scaffolding. "And these." He showed two photographs of the smashed body on the pavement. "Leather shoes, as we know from the inventory, with steel tips at toes and heels. If we believe just what we're expected to, he walked along that scaffolding and threw himself over—and steel didn't make a mark on the steel. You'd think there would be scratches somewhere, wouldn't you, even if he actually balanced himself on the middle of his soles before jumping."

The Divisional man said thinly: "You uncanny beggar."

"Nothing uncanny about it, just the facts speaking for themselves," said Roger mildly. "I could be way off beam, too—he might have jumped from another spot, but there was only this one steel scaffolding platform immediately above the place where he fell, so for our purpose we can assume he actually stood here. Well, why? There were wooden planks, making platforms at several spots. Why didn't he walk along one of those? Why walk along tubular steel, which is awkward going for anyone not used to it? You know, I think we'll have the body exhumed."

"*What?*"

"It might be as well to find out for sure how he

died," Roger murmured. "The injuries were so bad and the thing was so obvious that there might have been an oversight. Who did the p.m.?"

"Maddock."

"He'll love me for life after this," said Roger with a grimace, "especially if he finds anything he missed the first time. Millsom's buried in Chelsea, isn't he?"

"Yes."

"Listen," said Roger, "will you fix the exhumation, without bringing me into it, and keep it as quiet as you can?"

"Who's scaring you?" demanded the Divisional man. "Surely not Turnbull."

"I'd like to keep him off this for a bit."

"You'll have the Press on it like wolves," the other said.

Certainly they wouldn't be able to keep the news of an exhumation quiet for long. The Division would have to apply for an order, and the Press would soon hear of it, but if the job was done quickly, Roger would see the result of the second examination of the body before anyone tumbled to what was behind it. Maddock was a good pathologist, and wouldn't take any risks of making the same mistake twice.

It was little more than a shot in the dark; if it scored a hit, then a murderer was still free and they didn't yet know why Betty Gelibrand had been killed.

Luck turned Roger's way that afternoon.

Turnbull was sent North, following a request for Yard assistance from the Lake District, and the exhumation and second post-mortem were carried out while he was away. The Press was beaten comfortably. Plump, bald-headed Dr. Maddock himself, looking tired and glum, brought the result to Roger.

"He was probably suffocated before the time he was pushed off," Maddock growled. "Not much doubt, I'm afraid. I had Osborn with me. He spotted pressure marks on the throat and faint signs of suffocation on windpipe and throat. So did I, on making a better job. I've come a big cropper, didn't worry much about looking for anything else, the injuries seemed to speak for themselves. He couldn't have been dead long, the bleeding was so free that it suggested death on the impact; I was too damned cursory about the rest. My new report's going through. Maybe my resignation ought to go with it."

"Don't you resign," Roger said urgently. "If you want to take your punishment like a man, tell Turnbull all about it when he gets back. If you survive that you'll deserve to be kept on the payroll."

He was excited, but that didn't alter the fact that he had greater reason to be worried. Millsom had been a murderer's victim. Hidden by the platform, someone else had suffocated him and pushed him over; and Turnbull had missed it. Here was a case going sour on the younger officer. What would come of it?

Remember, though—Turnbull had saved his life.

There was a surge of activity at St. Cleo's. Yard and Divisional men virtually took the church over. The different approaches to the roof were checked, every inch was gone over thoroughly, every print was taken. It was a massive job. The workers on the rebuilding and repair were co-operative, and their prints were checked; prints were found of two people with small hands who could not be identified.

It was impossible to be sure when they had been made, but they were found on the approach to the roof from the inside, on two or three tools in the hut, and on sheltered pieces of scaffolding.

Photographs of these two sets of prints stood on Roger's desk.

Hundreds of people were questioned. Two or three remembered seeing young Millsom call at the vicarage. Others "thought" they had seen a small man go into the church when it was very late— "about" the time of the tragedy. Someone else was sure that a small woman dressed in gray had gone there one evening about the same time. Nothing was conclusive, but every trifling report was noted.

Throughout the upheaval, Millsom's father kept in the background. When it was over, Roger went to the vicarage to see him. The other's calm gray eyes had lost much of the hurt, but the Rev. Millsom seemed a rapidly aging man.

"Do you think my son innocent, Mr. West?"

"I think there might be doubt about his guilt," Roger said. "Once I'm sure, I'll let you know."

The clergyman nodded, as if satisfied; but how could he answer one inescapable question?

If he hadn't killed Betty, why had his son run away?

Questions of a different kind flung themselves at Roger. Who had been at St. Cleo's? Who had been on the roof? Who had killed Millsom, Betty Gelibrand, and Hilda Shaw? Had the two girls anything in common apart from beauty?

Roger searched all the records and found nothing except the fact that Hilda Shaw had also won a competition; he didn't yet know which one. He decided to make a visit to Tottenham his next call, and then his telephone bell rang.

That was at three o'clock on the afternoon following the exhumation. Chatworth had murmured congratulations, many men at the Yard felt stimulated, there were plenty of dry cracks at the still-absent Turnbull.

"Roger West here."

"Dalby here, Sergeants' Room," said a man briskly. "There's a job you might be interested in, sir. Girl's body found in the garden of an empty house at St. John's Wood. Hidden by bushes, been there about three weeks. The smell made a neighbor go and look. Would you like—"

"Wait for me," Roger said quietly. "I'll be in the hall in ten minutes. Know anything about her?"

"Not yet," Dalby said

It was literally impossible to guess anything from the girl's appearance; Roger didn't try. But her handbag was found in the bushes, there were snapshots, her address, oddments which gave him most of the information he wanted. Within two hours he was in a small front sitting room at a house in St. John's Wood, near Regent's Park. He had a glossy photograph of the dead girl in his hands; and beyond all doubt she was a beauty. The odd thing was to realize that she was dead; in the picture she looked so very much alive, radiant, happy.

Her mother was a faded beauty, with frightened eyes dulled with shock.

"Oh, I can't begin to tell you how I feel.... My Rose, my precious little Rose.... She was so happy when she won the competition, I've *never* seen her happier.... I couldn't do anything to disappoint her, when she rang up and said she wasn't coming home for a few days, I *couldn't* disappoint her, could I? She said it was one chance in a thousand, I couldn't ..."

She went on and on, unable to stop the flow. She moved about the room, touching things, picking them up, putting them down, then standing quite still and closing her eyes tightly, then moving again, still talking in that monotonous drawl.

"I can't believe it's happened to my Rose, she was such a good girl, I tell you she was a *good* girl. She might have made a few mistakes, but she wasn't flighty, not really flighty, and she was so *sure* she was going to be a success." The dazed woman paused. "A success, a success," she repeated brokenly. "And I think she would have been, too. How *could* she have failed? Look how lovely she is!"

Roger said: "Yes, I can see, Mrs. Alderson, she was a really beautiful girl, I don't wonder she was ambitious. What competition did she win?"

"Why, Conway's Beauty Competition, you know, Conway's Soap." Mrs. Alderson closed her eyes again, and stood with a hand pressed against a table. "I can't believe ..."

Roger's heart was thudding; a suffocating kind of beat. Here was the third dead beauty and another winner of a Conway's Beauty Competition. Just coincidence? That was unbelievable.

The woman stopped for a moment.

"Let me have any other photographs you have,"

Roger said gently, "we'll find the man who killed her, Mrs. Alderson."

She opened her gray eyes, and they blazed with a sudden fury.

"What good will that do, you fool?" she cried. "Will that bring my Rosy back? Go on, tell me, will it bring my Rosy back? She was the best daughter in the world, she was a good girl, *will catching the man bring her back?*"

Detective Sergeant Dalby was experienced and ready. He distracted her attention, and soon she quieted. Within an hour, Roger was slowing down outside a house near a park in Tottenham, a small house in a long row of small houses. A Divisional man was by his side.

"Want me, sir?" he asked.

"Just wait, will you?" Roger said.

He hurried to the front door, confident that there would be no distress here; the report which had not said which beauty contest she had won had described her mother as "outwardly indifferent."

A small, striking, middle-aged woman opened the door, started when she saw him; and then smiled warmly. Roger placed her in a second; that kind of smile was the same the whole world over, as was this kind of woman. She had a fine figure and dressed to improve it, and she had a face which gave meaning to seduction.

Roger was brusque.

When she realized that he was from the Yard, her manner changed, she became waspish.

"Look, why don't you forget all about it? We can't bring her back, can we? Anyone would think you policemen had nothing better to do than worry the life out of—"

"Had your daughter ever taken part in a Beauty Competition?" Roger broke in briskly. Pretended ignorance would serve best with this woman.

"Supposing she had."

"Had she?"

"'Course she had," declared Mrs. Shaw. "She won three the summer before last, two last year, never entered without getting in the first three. She only entered for one this year, and she was well on the way to winning it."

"Which one?" That was the vital question.

"The biggest *and* the best," boasted Mrs. Shaw. "Nothing but the best was good enough for my Hilda, if she hadn't lived up to that she might have been alive today. Conway's the soap people. She won their North London heat, and was in the finals—for a thousand-pound first prize. Or don't you fellows know *anything*?"

8

Big Prize

Conway's, an old-established corporation, spread their activities far beyond soaps, soap powder and detergents, and touched the fringes of many other preparations, including beauty and skin foods, toilet preparations, some pharmaceutical goods, and a wide range of toilet accessories. They ran the Beauty Queen of Britain Competition each year in association with a popular weekly magazine, which was controlled by Conway's. Roger found that there were always twelve district heats, and studied a map—issued as a Conway advertisement. This showed London divided into four districts, as well as five other English districts—South, Southwest, Midlands, Northwest, and Northeast—together with a district each in Scotland, Wales, and Northern Ireland. The winner from each heat would take part in the finals, later in the year. Victory carried a thousand pounds, the title of Miss Britain, the right to take part in a World Contest; and Conway's Queen would be given a great chance to break into the film world.

Roger talked to Chatworth...

"I don't think we want to tackle Conway's openly at this stage," he said, "but I'd like to get at someone reliable on the staff there, someone who has a bit to do with organizing the competitions." He still felt the tension of excitement which had come with the discovery of a connecting factor among the three murders. "We're only on the fringe of it yet, sir, but—" he paused.

"Well, go on."

"There've been seven heats so far, three in London, one in the South of England, one Northwest, one Northeast, one Midlands," Roger said. "The three London winners are now dead. It would be easy to say that pretty girls who win Beauty Competitions sometimes lose their heads and get themselves into trouble, but—"

"For once I'm not arguing with you," Chatworth interrupted. "This isn't coincidence, and nothing's going to make me believe it is. Watch those other four winners. Check arrangements for other district competitions. Spend all your time on this unless something urgent crops up. See all the girls, get their photographs—oh, go away and stop grinning, you know what to do!"

Roger jumped up.

"Oh, Turnbull's on his way back," Chatworth said. "Had quite a triumph up there. I had the Chief Constable on the telephone an hour ago—says that Turnbull did a brilliant job and finished in three days when anyone else would have taken a week. Want him on this job?"

"It's up to you," Roger said.

It would be an object lesson to see how Turnbull took the rebuff that he was going to walk into. Did he know about the exhumation and the finding, or had he been too preoccupied with the case in Westmorland?

Oh, forget him. Three Beauty Queens had been murdered during the past seven—no, nine weeks, he was forgetting his two weeks out of action. Four Queens might be in danger, and five more heats were due to be run before the summer was out. Watching the new winners would become priority for the Divisions and County Police concerned and none would take it lightly.

It was easy to get information, names, and addresses of all the heat winners and runners-up from the magazine. The London Divisions and County Police were told, and the four Queens quietly watched.

Roger was studying every minute detail of the competitions when Turnbull came into the office.

Only Eddie Day was present.

Turnbull came in quietly, yet it was still quite an entrance. Roger looked around. The Detective Inspector was not smiling so broadly as usual; there was tension in his manner. He had his hat on, tipped to one side, and his brown suit was perfectly cut.

He nodded to Eddie, walked straight to Roger.

"Hallo. They tell me you've been busy."

"This and that turned up," Roger said.

"And I was a ruddy fool not to see them coming. Made me quite a spectacle for everyone to laugh at." There was no real feeling in Turnbull's voice, and he seemed shaken. "Good job you came back

71

on duty when you did, or everything might have been forgotten."

"We don't forget easily," Roger said.

"So we don't." Turnbull took off his hat, and spun it round on his forefinger deftly. Round and round, round and round. "I see what you mean. Any objection if I keep on the case with you?"

"Not up to me," Roger murmured.

"You can say the word, and Chatworth will assign me to the job," Turnbull said. "Or you can tell him I've been a loudmouthed braggart with the wrong sense of smell, and keep me off it. Which are you going to do?"

"If you want it and you can be spared for the job, I won't try to keep you off," Roger told him. He glanced at Eddie, then moved toward the door. "There are one or two things in *Records* I want to show you." He led the way out, and in the passage went on very quietly, "Never mind *Records*, we'll find a corner in the canteen, I want to talk to you."

"The maestro about to give a lesson?"

Roger said deliberately, "Listen, Turnbull, I don't want an argument. I'm not interested in giving you or anyone else lessons." They walked side by side toward the stairs, Turnbull an inch taller, an inch broader; two massive men. Roger walked with a slight limp, because his leg was still bandaged. Two or three men passed them before they reached the canteen and found a corner away from everyone else. "No need for Eddie Day, Chatworth, or anyone else to be in on this one," Roger went on deliberately, and offered cigarettes.

"Thanks." Turnbull flicked a lighter. "What's so important that it needs a conspiracy?"

"You flopped on the Gelibrand job, and you want

72

to make up for it," Roger said. "That kind of thing has happened to all of us, and will keep happening. Any man here with a hundred per cent record would have wings and a halo, but I've never seen any. How much do you know about it now?"

"Beauty Queen mystery," said Turnbull.

"That's it. Remember coming back from Telham the day we'd seen Betty Gelibrand? We were stuck in a traffic jam near Victoria. A woman passed along the pavement, and you demonstrated what a fine wolf whistle you've got?"

Turnbull was clenching his hands tightly.

"So what?"

"You could go wrong again on this job, missing the wood for the trees. Or the killer of luscious lovelies." The attempt to be flippant failed miserably; Roger wished he'd never made it. It wasn't easy to do the right thing with Turnbull, because Turnbull was so obviously suspicious of a trick; of being fooled. "And you'll be so anxious to make amends that you might overreach yourself again."

"What exactly are you saying, West?" No "Handsome"; no friendliness; just a cool voice and a hard stare. "That I'll fall for a skirt and forget the job?"

"I'm saying you can't afford to go wrong on this one again, and if there's anything in it that makes you think you might go wrong, you ought to keep off. I shan't do anything to make you."

"Just a friendly warning," Turnbull said, and sneered.

Then suddenly, unexpectedly, he laughed and clapped Roger on the shoulder. His face cleared, his voice became deep, amiable.

"Okay, okay, Handsome! I'm dim-witted today, perhaps I'm dim-witted all the time! I thought you

73

were taking a rise out of me, instead of that you're doing me a favor. Thanks a million! I'll think it over—not that I'm worried about being put off the scent by a nice piece of goods. Imagine you remembering that floosie in Victoria Street. There's more to you even than I thought!" He laughed again, and seemed much more natural. "You're a lucky man in other ways too, aren't you?"

"Am I?"

"Two fine kids and a beautiful wife!"

"What do you want me to do?" Roger asked. "Find you a nice girl to settle down with?"

They laughed ...

Things weren't quite right between them, all the same. Turnbull had changed his attitude, probably because he had realized that he was adopting a bad one, but he hadn't felt as lighthearted as he'd tried to sound. Roger hoped he would not have to work with him, but was reluctant to do anything to keep him off the case. He owed Turnbull too much.

Next morning, Chatworth telephoned him. "Conway's managing director has just been on the phone to me," he said. "Wants to know if we'd like the competition heats suspended. Would you?"

"No!" Roger almost blurted.

"Might pick up a thing or two from them, eh?"

"Well, it's possible," Roger said more cautiously.

"I'll just say 'not yet,'" Chatworth promised. "Oh, another thing. Unless you've thought of any strong objection, I'm going to have Turnbull working with you on this job," he said. "He seems to see it as a test case."

Roger said flatly, "Very good, sir."

*   *   *

"My, my, my," exclaimed Turnbull, looking down at the photographs placed out on Roger's desk. "Seven of the best. Pity about those two, they've got a slight edge on the others, I fancy. Don't you?" He pointed to photographs of Betty Gelibrand and Hilda Shaw. "Not that the others would make me want to run home to mama." He seemed to be talking a little too fast and for the sake of it. "Seen the others in the flesh yet?"

"No. We're making the rounds today."

"It can't be too soon for me! What do you make of it, Handsome? I've been trying to catch up on everything so that I'll know what you're talking about. Conway's are running this series of Beauty Contests up and down the country, and the big prize is worth one thousand jimmy o' goblins with a chance of a three-year contract in the films."

"That's it," Roger said.

"So it's worth a possible three or four thousand pounds."

"Easily."

"Lots of murders have been committed for less than three thousand pounds," said Turnbull. "Now tell me I'm jumping to conclusions again, and I'll agree. Still, it's an angle. Look for the beauty who would bump off all the other beauties so that she's got an easy passage to the first prize."

He grinned.

"I've been at the Yard so long I can believe anything," Roger said dryly. "The fact that we're working together on this doesn't mean that we have to be together all the time." He waved at the four photographs of living girls. "Take your choice of

75

two, and find out what you can about the competition they won, will you?"

"Looking for a factor common to them all?"

"Looking for anything that doesn't fit in the way things should fit in."

"Okay. And then?"

"Then we'll watch the new competitions wherever they're staged," said Roger, "and check the new winners. The final's due at Blackpool in the autumn. If there is a final! Conway's made an offer to call it off this morning—they spoke to the A.C."

"Turned it down?" Turnbull asked sharply.

"Yes—for the time being, anyhow. This way, we do know where the danger might be."

"Do we! We're going to have ourselves a time," went on Turnbull, and grinned, obviously approving. "Forgetting Beauty Queens, mind if I take your kids out one of these days? Lord's or the Oval, say."

"Nice of you," said Roger. "Why not?" It was a handsome olive branch, but neither that nor anything else could make them really friendly; it was hard to put a finger on the reason.

Roger saw two of the other Queens. They were nice-looking girls, but not so outstanding as two of the dead girls.

Turnbull came back from his reconnaissance, grinning with almost satyrish delight.

"Did I pick the winner, Handsome! One of them was just another sweetie pie, but the other—pheee-oooh! I've never seen anything on two legs and *terra firma* to match it. And believe me, I'm a connoisseur. Wait until you see her."

Roger, meanwhile, received reports on the chief organizers of the competitions. There were three men and a girl. Three, including the girl, worked for Conway's, the other for Pomerall's, the advertising agents who had thought up the competition.

All of them would be at a Hammersmith Dance Hall that week for the West London Competition.

Roger and Turnbull had seats near the front of the big hall. Two thousand fans were sitting round the sides. Fifty girls in swim suits stood in the center, most with praiseworthy grace and composure, and each moved forward to be inspected critically, told to prance up and down, expected to preen herself.

Roger picked out the three men who worked regularly on the competition.

Derek Talbot, sleek, long-haired, wiry yet oddly effeminate, good-looking in an almost feline way, sat with a local civic dignitary and two budding film stars, as advisers to the "bench." Ushering the girls before the "bench" was a different kind of man altogether, large, ruggedly good-looking, obviously an outdoor man. He was the compère, Mark Osborn; he was also the advertising agency member.

The third man was a different type again, older, quiet, always in the background.

Turnbull had also been probing, and pointed the man out: "Wilfrid Dickerson," he said, "with the best job of the lot! He has to check their measurements, all the girls have to be within a schedule. Believe it or not, the lovelies prefer a man; they seem to think that a woman would swindle them."

Dickerson looked gray, aging, tired.

"I'm told he can tell a fake figure at a glance," Turnbull grinned. "Amazing what they'll get up to, isn't it? Dickerson's good on facts, anyway—

knows the soap business backward and forward. Who wouldn't take soap as a lifetime's study, if it leads to measuring luscious lovelies?"

"Where's the secretary to the group?" asked Roger, dryly.

"The mousy one," Turnbull said, pointing to a girl near Dickerson. "Hard to believe she's got a figure at all. I—"

He broke off, staring.

A latecomer hurried to join the competitors, and sight of her silenced Turnbull completely. She made Roger draw in his breath sharply, too.

She moved with a grace which caught everyone's attention. She was raven-haired, and had a skin that looked so perfect that it could hardly be real. True beauty was in her manner, her unselfconscious walk, and smile and actions. She seemed completely natural. No other competitor had a chance against her; that seemed positive from the moment she appeared.

Turnbull kept staring at her.

"There's the lassie for my money," he said very softly.

Roger thought, "I oughtn't to have had you on this job."

It was too late to do anything about that now.

9

Regina Howard

Regina Howard put her lipstick into her handbag late on the evening of the day after she had won the Hammersmith Competition. She was in her office, one of a small suite in the same building as Conway's, in Bennis Square, Mayfair, W.1., and was secretary and general factotum of a small fashion agency, pleasant work if not highly paid. The proprietor was seldom in the office, so she was virtually in charge.

The Competition office was on this floor, and Derek Talbot and Mark Osborn kept finding excuses for looking in. Now it was Talbot.

"No, Derek, I can't dine with you tonight. I'm tired, and there's a lot to do," she said firmly. "So I'll eat at home."

"*Avec* invalid mother?"

"Can you think of any good reason why not?"

"But, my darling," cried Talbot, "I can think of a hundred good reasons why you shouldn't stay in a frowsty flat on a glorious evening in July. You should celebrate last night's resounding victory—

which was always inevitable. And the best way to celebrate is to come for a spin with your humble servant. We ought to dine at Maidenhead or somewhere by the river, then take out a boat. My word on it, I shall not make a single attempt to sully your honor!"

Regina laughed.

"I don't think you would, either, and it sounds heavenly, but no, I can't."

"Can't? Won't? Is the *mère* the reason or the excuse to give me the brush-off every time, old gel?"

Talbot had a pleasant voice, a pleasant face, hair which was a little too wavy for a man and a little too long. His clothes were a little too perfect, too. He was tall, slim, svelte. He had once had ambition to paint, but too little energy to carry it out, and had drifted into the Conway Organization through its Art Department, designing show cards and packing cartons, and had become the chief liaison with Pomerall & Pomerall, Advertising Agents. With his opposite number at Pomerall's, the rugged Mark Osborn, he had hatched the Beauty Competition scheme which was catching the eye of the public as few schemes had done before. Both men were in high favor with their respective boards of directors; both were on the crest of a wave.

Both had known Regina Howard for several months, too, and Talbot had urged her to enter for the West London Competition. She hadn't been keen, but his and her mother's persuasion had succeeded. Mark Osborn hadn't made much comment.

"Well, is it reason or excuse?" Talbot demanded.

"Don't be silly, Derek," Regina sounded absent-minded.

"Dear old pulchritude," Talbot said sweetly, "I can't help being the addle-pate champion of the world. But now and again glimmerings of the old maternal intelligence show up. I mean, substitute Mark for *mère*. Would I be right?"

Regina stopped by the door of her office, turned and looked fully into the sallow face, and said quite simply, "Derek, if I was going out with Mark and couldn't see you because of it, I'd say so."

Talbot gulped.

"Oh, lor'! Old foot in the old soup again. Of course you would. Apologies for base suspicions. Blame my infernal internal jealousy. In case I forgot to tell you yesterday, I love you. Passionately, deliriously, wholly, possessively. I think," continued Derek Talbot, and gave his most gentle smile, "that I would break the neck of any man who threatened to march you off to the altar. Or poison him, or stick a knife in his ribs."

They walked in silence to the lift. It was empty. The building was large, modern, sumptuous. Now, at half-past six, only a few office workers were there, and some early cleaners. Somewhere a vacuum was humming; otherwise there was no sound.

The door closed hissingly behind them, enclosing them in the shiny solitude of the walnut-veneered lift. Derek Talbot pressed the ground-floor button.

"The horrible thing about that remark of yours," said Regina, very slowly, "is that you probably mean it."

"Oh, I do. You have been warned."

"Derek, I—"

"Say no more, lady," said Talbot brightly. He slid his arm about her shoulders and gave her a little

81

hug. "See how brotherly I can be toward the wonderful woman who is so full of sisterly love for me." He kissed her lightly on the forehead. "As I live," he declared, "I don't think Mark's the right man for you."

"As I live," said Regina, trying to make herself sound lighthearted, "I don't think I've met the right man."

They came to a stop.

"Give you a lift anywhere, ma'am?" asked Talbot, brightly. Outside, he dropped his flippancy, and said quietly, "No regrets, Gina, have you?"

"About what?"

"The competition."

She said slowly: "I don't really know. I was never too keen to enter, and now I've won this heat, I'm not sure I want to go on."

"The idiot conscience?"

"Well, *is* it fair that I know you and Mark *and* Dickerson? You can influence—"

"Hold it," Talbot broke in. "The judges are completely independent. If I'd breathed a word in your favor, they'd almost certainly have turned you down. No word was needed, anyhow. You were streets ahead. If I mean streets! And you will be in the final, too. Give yourself a chance, Gina. Why, even your mother wants you to take this one!"

"I'll think it over," Regina said. "Thanks, Derek."

Hers was a very little car. She graced it as she graced everything. Her movements, as she stooped to get inside, had a supple ease. Talbot stood on the pavement of Bennis Square and watched her move off; soon the little car was lost in a stream of traffic.

He turned away....

Regina Howard was compelled to drive in line, and for ten minutes she crawled along, and had time to think. Derek worried her. He was too intense by far, there were moments when he almost scared her. One could never be quite sure what his mood would be. The flippancy tonight might well be replaced by an almost vicious, hurtful sarcasm tomorrow. It hadn't always been like that; this moodiness was something which had developed during the past few months. She didn't then connect it with the Beauty Competition, because that was just part of his job, and he always seemed completely happy about it. He let nothing interfere with work. The truth about Derek, she reflected as the traffic began to thin out, was that he was ruthless; much more ruthless than most people would suspect. They were fooled by his almost effeminate manners and his fastidiousness in dress into thinking that he was weak willed. Weak—Derek Talbot!

He wanted her to win the final, was absurdly sure that she would, if she went on.

Mark Osborn, who looked a he-man, was much the weaker character in some ways; irresolute over many things. Her, for instance. Yet of the two she preferred Mark and was more content in his company. She had even been wondering if she ought to marry him. That had been in her mind all day—because of a completely new element, a disturbing one she couldn't understand. Last night at Hammersmith she had seen a man who had almost hypnotized her. A powerful, imposing giant...

She shared a small West London flat with a semi-invalid mother, in a street near the Edgware Road. The houses were tall and narrow, gray-fronted, pleasant. This was a tree-lined backwater, extremely convenient and not too expensive.

She turned the corner, and involuntarily her foot went on the brake.

A low-lying scarlet M.G. stood outside the door of Number 27, her house. That was Mark Osborn's car. He hadn't said that he would be calling, she hadn't expected him. Her thoughts flashed to Derek; if he saw the car here, he would think that she was a liar, and that wouldn't help the future relationship. It would affect both Derek and Mark, too. They worked together so closely that any estrangement could only be harmful.

She pulled up behind the M.G.

The front door, as always, was unlatched. Hers was the ground-floor flat. As she unlocked and opened the door, she heard her mother say:

"I'm sure she won't be long, Mr. Osborn, if she's going to be very late she always telephones me."

"Trust Gina," said Mark, in his deep, powerful, and deceptive voice. "Hallo, what's this?" There were footsteps, and then he appeared at the door of the living room. His broad, rugged face lit up. "Why, hallo, old girl. Been waiting for you!"

"I can't imagine why," Regina said dryly.

"As a matter of fact I want a little chat," Mark said. "Believe it or not, it's about business. And your mother says that she'll forgive me if I carry you off to dinner."

"Of course, dear," Mrs. Howard said.

She was Regina's height and coloring, she was going gray, and there was a bluish tinge at her lips, sign of an obscure heart complaint. She was subject to fainting fits, too, but none of these things affected her as much as her one great affliction.

The right side of her face was paralyzed.

The tragedy of this only became fully apparent when one saw the profile of the left side of her face, which was quite beautiful, even now. That side was normal, too; when she talked her lips moved, she could blink—anyone looking from that side would notice nothing. The right side was like a distorted beauty mask.

She hated to meet strangers, because of this, and seldom went out. But both Derek Talbot and Mark Osborn had met her several times, and she had close friends among the neighbors.

Regina, having lived with the situation, often forgot there was anything the matter with the older woman. Now she remembered Derek's expression when he had asked if her mother was the excuse for her refusal. So much reminded her of Derek. On the table was a fresh box of chocolates, and she felt sure they were from him.

Mark looked at her steadily. It was difficult to understand him in this mood. Usually his eyes were just clear and friendly. Now, they were cloudy, scared—frightened? He was silently pleading with her to accept.

"Well, if it's important, I'd love to come," Regina said.

The moment she said that she realized that it sounded graceless, but Mark didn't seem to notice.

As they drove off, he asked if she were sure her mother would be all right.

"Oh, yes," Regina said, "if she gets lonely she'll go along the street to a neighbor's."

"She does go out sometimes, then."

"Not often." It was odd that Mark should want to talk about that, but there was no reason why she

85

shouldn't encourage him. "She's very sensitive, of course."

"Has she always been like it?"

"No," Regina said, "it was an accident while climbing in Switzerland. My father slipped, and they both fell. He died. She was paralyzed for a year, and gradually recovered except for her face."

"Oh, shocking bad luck," Mark said. "I shouldn't have talked about it, but—"

"It's all right, Mark," Regina assured him.

Somehow, it had eased the tension she had felt.

Derek certainly wasn't likely to see her here with Mark; that shouldn't matter, but it did. The restaurant was in a little side street near Paddington Station, the last place Regina would have looked for one. From the outside it was just a big window, a small window, and a green-painted door with faded wording on the fascia board above it. Inside, it was pleasant; red-plush seats round the walls, red-seated chairs on the other side, little tables with spotless white damask and glistening silver —a pleasant place indeed. Soft-footed, dark-skinned waiters moved about, speaking barely intelligible English in a variety of accents.

A coffee-colored man had greeted them and taken their order, making it obvious that he knew Mark.

"It's rather nice," Regina said. "How often do you come here?"

"Oh, now and then," Mark answered. "Found it by accident a couple of years ago. Not bad." He spoke rather jerkily.

Regina was quite sure that he had a great weight on his mind, and was afraid that she knew what it was. This was going to be a proposal. Mark had screwed himself up to storm the flat, win her mother over, and virtually force her into spending the evening with him. "Business" was a blind. She wished it hadn't happened. He looked so massive and strong, but she knew that he could be hurt at least as easily as Derek.

She didn't say anything to help him.

The food was very good indeed.

She took coffee but not a liqueur. Mark had brandy in a big glass, and a cigar. As the time approached for talking he looked more and more ill-at-ease; and yet when he burst out with the subject, he took her completely by surprise.

"Gina," he said, "I'm scared. *Badly* worried. You haven't noticed anything, have you?"

She didn't answer, just looked bewildered.

"Shouldn't have blurted it at you like that," Mark said, "but—well, it had to come out. And obviously you haven't noticed a thing."

She fumbled for a cigarette.

"I don't understand, Mark."

"Hell of a thing to have to say," Mark muttered, and licked his lips. "At first I thought I was crazy, but now I'm pretty sure that I'm right. In fact, I'm quite sure, and the police have discovered it, too."

Regina said: "Give me a light, Mark, and stop being mysterious."

"Eh? Oh, a light. Sorry!" A match scraped. His hand was steady as he held it out to her. "Hell of a situation. You know all about Betty Gelibrand, of course, the South London winner—poor kid."

Regina felt as if a door had opened and a cold wind had blown in; that was partly due to Mark's manner, partly due to vague thoughts that had been at the back of her own mind.

87

"Yes," she said.

"Then there was Hilda Shaw. Hilda was one of the first winners. I must have mentioned her to you."

Regina said stiffly: "Yes, I—I saw her photograph. You and Derek—"

She broke off.

"I know," said Mark. "We were showing you what you'd have to compete with if you reached the final. Hell, you know almost as much as we do about the competition! First, there was Betty Gelibrand. Murdered. There was a big fuss in the papers, and a chap threw himself off the roof to stop himself being caught for her murder. Remember?"

"Of course."

"I was reading in the *Globe* that the police believe he also murdered Hilda Shaw," Mark went on, cupping his brandy glass and looking searchingly into Regina's eyes. "Now I've come up against a third."

Regina just felt as if the wind were getting colder, and that she would soon begin to shiver.

"Rose Alderson's dead, too," Mark said abruptly. "Her body was found in some bushes in the garden of a house in St. John's Wood. That's *three* of them. It was in the papers the day before yesterday, but the police were cagey, and her name didn't appear. It's in the evening papers tonight, though, with a photograph of Rose. Couldn't be anyone else. That's *three* winners dead."

The shiver came to Regina.

"You—you see what I mean?" Mark muttered.

Regina had to say something, but didn't know what to say that would make any sense. The thing

88

which most worried her was the genuine fear in Mark's eyes; as if he was frightened by some suspicions, some knowledge, something more than the simple facts.

"I think I see what you mean," Regina made herself say. "Three of them—"

"It's hell!" Mark burst out. "It's as if we select a winner and point a finger at her, and then someone comes along and kills her. And now you've won—"

"Mark, don't be silly, and keep your voice low!"

He gulped again. "Well, isn't it all true?"

"I think you're being slightly neurotic," Regina said, very clearly and distinctly. "These girls often do lose their heads, success spoils them, and—"

"It's no use trying to rationalize it," Mark said. "I've done that for some time—now Rose Alderson's gone, I've stopped. Someone's setting out to kill our winners. God, it's dreadful. And—the police are on to it."

Regina made herself say, "Well, if it's true, it's time they were."

He lifted the glass suddenly, drank some brandy, let the glass go down heavily on the table.

"Oh, I suppose you're right, but I've got the jitters. I've been followed for the last twenty-four hours. So's Derek. So have you. Two men from Scotland Yard were at Hammersmith last night. But the police haven't said much to the firm, as far as I know, and they haven't questioned anyone directly. They're just snooping, and I don't like it."

"But if it's the best way for them to find out what's happening—"

"Listen," said Mark, and gripped her wrists; she was surprised that his fingers were so hard and so cold. "That chap who threw himself off the church roof could have killed all of them. Rose's body was lying in the bushes for over three weeks. But if the police thought he'd killed them, why would they be snooping around us? Whom do they suspect? Why follow you and me? I tell you I'm scared stiff, I just can't take it. It wouldn't be so bad if they'd come out in the open with questions, but this constant watching is getting me down. I—"

Mark Osborn stopped abruptly.

Someone had just come in, and was approaching the table. He looked up, and saw Derek Talbot. Regina looked round swiftly, saw Derek, and felt a flame of alarm at the glitter in his eyes.

10

Drunk Derek

Derek was drunk.

It showed in his unsteady poise, loose mouth, glittering eyes—bloodshot, angry eyes. He made straight for the table, pushing aside the olive-skinned head waiter. Two other waiters moved forward swiftly, but something in Derek's manner kept them back.

"Please, m'sieur," began the head waiter despairingly.

"Wish to say," said Derek, abruptly.

He didn't finish, but reached the table and stood staring down. He looked at Regina, not at Mark. Everyone else in the room stared at him, at least two men moved protectingly in front of their women.

"Derek, don't make a scene here," Regina pleaded quickly, quietly. "I can explain and—"

"Silence!" Derek raised a hand, like a traffic policeman stopping oncoming traffic. "Wish to say"—he belched ever so slightly, and moved his hand to pat his lips—"all women are deceivers ever. Old

91

saw wrong way round. Don't like being made fool of, don't like being lied to, don't like—"

He spun round and aimed a sweeping blow at Mark.

Regina followed the movement of his hand, saw Mark's involuntary movement and his failure to dodge the blow, which caught him sharply on the right cheek. Someone cried out, and one of the waiters made an indeterminate movement forward. Regina felt that there wasn't a thing she could do, knew that everyone was staring at her— and then saw Mark jump up. He moved in a single swift movement, jolting the table, knocking the ashtray off. One of his fists buried itself in Derek's stomach, the other flashed upward to his chin.

She actually saw Derek's eyes roll before they closed, and he crumpled up.

"Sorry about this," Mark said, and somehow managed to stop Derek from falling. "My friend's not well," he added to a waiter. "Come on, Gina." He moved very quickly, sliding an arm round Derek's waist, then placing Derek's arm round his shoulder. "I'll be in tomorrow," he said to the waiter.

"Of course, sir, whenever you like."

Regina picked up her wrap and mesh handbag, saw Mark's cigarette case on the table and picked it up, then hurried after him. He was carrying Derek quite smoothly and easily, as if he was used to handling drunks. The head waiter reached the door and opened it.

The light fell onto the dingy street and onto a man who stood opposite.

He was big and brashly imposing. Regina had seen him at the Hammersmith Competition the night before, and had felt an almost hypnotic influence of his brown eyes, hadn't found it easy to look away.

He smiled at her, boldly.

Mark didn't appear to notice him, but dragged Derek to the M.G. No other car was near.

"Have to squeeze him in the back," he said. "Idiot's as tight as a drum. Mind his legs." Doing things like this, Mark was astonishingly practical and competent, and he needed no help. "Have to drop you first, then I'll take him home," he went on. "What was he burbling about, do you know?"

Regina didn't answer.

Mark was already at the wheel.

"So you do," he said. "Have a hell of a time between the two of us, don't you?" She saw that he wasn't smiling. They passed beneath a street lamp, and then turned a corner. A moment later, Mark went on, "We're being followed, I thought someone was watching the restaurant. This is the thing that scares me—"

"You didn't act scared when Derek came in!"

"First thing a man should do is know himself," Mark said. He shot a glance at her, and in light from a shop window he saw that she was smiling. "Give me action and I'm as right as a trivet, I never could sit back and wait for anything. Next time I see that copper I shall probably punch him on the nose."

"That wouldn't help."

"It would ease my feelings," Mark said, with his gaze on the driving mirror again.

Regina wouldn't let him get out of the car and open the door for her, but watched the dark shape moving off; and she saw a car pass the end of a street a moment later; so Mark and Derek were being followed.

She put her own car away in a nearby garage, came back, and inserted her key in the front door.

She pushed it open, slowly; and it creaked a little.

She held her breath....

Silent darkness greeted her; only the remembered sound of the creaking door was in her ears. Yet she could not force herself to go in. Terror clutched her. She stood with a hand on the door, holding so tightly that her fingers hurt, and she looked into the blackness.

Then she heard another creak.

She opened her mouth and a sound grated in her throat; she went icy cold from head to foot, and shivered.

A light went on.

"Is that you, dear?" called her mother.

Regina slept.

It had been a little after midnight when she had got into bed, almost recovered from the absurd terror which had no positive cause, only an accumulation of causes with Mark's manner superimposed upon it. The one thing above all others which had bitten into her mind and heart was Mark's almost neurotic thought: "It's as if we select a winner and point a finger at her, and then someone comes along and kills her."

She had felt the same kind of thing, almost as if someone had whispered it to her, before he had talked of it. The murder of Hilda Shaw had made her regretful, but she hadn't known the girl well; or particularly liked her. Betty Gelibrand's death had upset her badly. At that stage she had felt simply as if fate were against them; as if some evil influence, some voodoo, lay upon the girls who won the competitions. One could argue, reject such thoughts as crazy, set oneself firmly against them—and they would persist. Not until now, though, had she known about Rose Alderson. She'd met the girl twice. Rose had been a perkily pretty little thing; a girl to like.

Mark and Derek, between them, had affected Regina so much that she had been shivering with icy fear when her mother had called out. Unreasoning, illogical fears began to possess her, as they possessed Mark. Mark was obviously living on his nerves; and so was Derek. Derek chose to seize upon his love for her as the excuse, but it wasn't the reason; it couldn't be the only reason, anyhow.

Was he scared, too?

It was a long time before Regina slept. Her small bedroom was next to her mother's, and at the back of the house. A window opened onto a little alley, which led from the back garden. On one side of the alley was the kitchen and the scullery. It was just large enough, pleasantly furnished, and—home.

So she slept at last, without dreaming.

By four o'clock, dawn was rousing the birds for their brief song, the east promised a bright glow of another fine day. It was already warm. Regina lay with her back to the window, breathing evenly, one arm bare to the shoulder and over the bedspread. The light was good enough, now, for her dark hair to show on the pillow.

There was a sound outside, but it did not disturb her.

A man crept toward the window.

He reached it, and stood with his face pressed against it, as if trying to make sure whether she was in bed. From where he stood, he could see her. He moved his hands, and drew a scarf over his face, so that only his eyes were clear. His hat, a trilby, was pulled low over his forehead.

He lowered his hands to the window.

He could not get his fingers beneath it, so he withdrew his hands, and took a small screwdriver from his pocket. He levered the window up far enough to get his fingers beneath it, and then pushed.

The window made a little grating sound.

Regina stirred.

The man pushed the window farther up, when she had stopped, and this time it did not appear to disturb her. There was no wind. Thick net curtains had moved up with the lower part of the window, and all he had to do was step over the sill and into the room.

He put one leg inside.

A moment later he stood by the side of Regina, looking down at her; and in the shadowy room he could just make out the shape outlined on the bed, and her arm, and her dark hair. He thrust his hands forward slowly, the gloved fingers crooked, and they moved toward her throat.

He bent down.

His hands were only a foot away from her; one swoop, and he could clutch her and choke the sound of fear away, squeeze until life went.

He crouched closer.

She breathed evenly, peacefully, her back still toward the window, the one arm bare and shapely against the green bedspread.

His fingers clutched at her throat.

She felt the sudden tightness, and woke on fire with a fear which seemed to scorch her heart, scorch her whole body. She was shaken by wild thumping, which smashed awfully against her breast. Then she realized that hands were choking her, that she couldn't breathe. She struck at the arms, touched but could not dislodge them. She could see the glitter of a pair of eyes.

She could see death.

Then a sound came from the alley, short and sharp, footsteps followed it. The man who was choking her turned away swiftly, and his pressure relaxed. She saw him, crouching and facing the window—and she heard the footsteps and a man call out, "Who's there?"

The man who had nearly choked her didn't speak, but jerked himself upright and streaked toward the door. Regina screamed, but the sound was shrill and weak. The man from outside reached the window, she saw that as she twisted round in bed. Then he thrust a leg through and climbed in. He was big and massive; that was all she noticed, because she was so afraid.

The room door opened, her assailant slammed it behind him. He raced along the passage, and she could hear his footsteps clearly. The big man was in the room now.

"All safe," he said, "don't worry, stay there!"

He reached the door in two long strides, opened it, and rushed out. Then Regina heard a new sound, heard him swear, and heard the roar of a shot.

She couldn't move.

"Ruddy swine," roared her rescuer.

She heard him moving, didn't know whether he was hurt. For the first time since she had woken, she felt that she could move. She pushed the bedclothes back and slid out of bed, waiting breathlessly, expecting the sound of another shot. It didn't come, but suddenly a door banged, and then a whistle shrilled out very loudly, up and down the street.

She reached the door.

A big man stood in the doorway with his back to her, and she thought that he was holding the whistle to his lips. It sounded again, ear-splitting, hateful. Then he turned round, and looked at her.

He was the big man who had been at the Hammersmith Competition; and who had been outside the restaurant, smiling at her in that bold, possessive way.

11

Turnbull Reports

Now there were sounds from upstairs and from the street; thumping on the floor above, voices in the house and outside; and the engine of a car, roaring.

The big man looked Regina up and down. He made her realize that she was wearing a filmy nightdress, caught up at the waist, sleeveless, more pretty than serviceable. She fought against the curious power which he seemed to exert over her, and said in a thin voice:

"Keep them quiet, they mustn't frighten my mother. Please!" She turned to her mother's door, and listened intently. She heard nothing.

A door leading from the flat above opened, the man began to talk in a quiet, commanding voice. Another man spoke from the front door, the night was full of voices.

Regina peered into the bedroom.

She could just make out the limp figure on the bed, lying on her good side; and Mrs. Howard was stone deaf in the ear in the paralyzed side of her face.

Regina closed the door quickly but softly, then turned back to her own room. Her heart was beating fast, but she felt much better; no longer terrified. She picked up a dressing gown, and started to put it on; then found that one sleeve was inside out.

She'd heard no footsteps, but the big man said, "Want some help?"

He was just behind her, and held the dressing gown out. She slipped her arms into it, and the man's hands held her shoulders for a split second, then let go. She tied the sash quickly, and turned to face him. She was flushed, and knew it, and she didn't know what to say.

He smiled at her with that bold, openly admiring smile.

"You're okay," he said, "and you'll do." Quite casually he looked at a box of chocolates on the dressing table, then said, "Mind?"

"No—no, of course not."

"Thanks." He took one, and as he did so a woman shouted from the passage:

"But I heard a shot, I tell you!"

The big man turned and disappeared. His voice was little more than a whisper, but it penetrated to every corner.

"Less noise, please, there's a sick woman in that room. Yes, ma'am, it was a shot, and we'll have the gunman before the sun's much higher. Be good enough to return to your flat and wait until we come for a statement, please." He was commandingly dominant, and gave the impression that he knew that everyone would obey him.

Everyone did, including two police constables who had arrived.

Regina listened....

She learned that the assailant had turned the nearest corner, toward a network of streets; it would have been a waste of time chasing him. She heard that the big man had already put police patrol cars on the hunt, and that one of the policemen had spoken to the Yard and also to his own Division. She got the impression that everything was completely under control.

The big man finished with everyone else, and turned to her.

"I don't want to be a nuisance, Miss Howard, but my men will have to look for fingerprints and clues and things." He grinned. "Mind?"

"I can't, can I?"

"They won't be long." Turnbull gave instructions, and two men took their equipment into her room. "And I'll have to ask you a few questions," he went on. "Nonsensical, the way we police behave, isn't it?" The grin came again. "How about a cup of tea while you're telling me."

A cup of tea was exactly what she needed.

"Oh, that's a good idea! I'll put a kettle on."

He followed her into the kitchen. There was nothing furtive about it. A policeman was in the yard, looking for clues; another was at the front door. This man seemed to be in no hurry, and he perched himself on the corner of the big deal kitchen table, watching her with that open admiration, making her feel a little uneasy; self-conscious, perhaps. Yet he made himself so completely at home.

"Time I told you who I am," he said. "Warren Turnbull, of the Yard." He seemed to think that she

101

would recognize the name at once; she did, but only vaguely, and couldn't bring herself to say so.

"Oh, *are* you?"

"At your service," said Turnbull. "I've been keeping an eye on you. Don't tell me you didn't know!"

"I—I've seen you about."

"Know who I was?"

"I believed—you were a policeman."

"Detective Inspector," he corrected, with unmistakable emphasis. "Now just tell me what happened tonight, will you? I don't mean just this past half-hour, I mean from the time you left here with Mark Osborn."

So he knew about that.

She began to talk, and was quite sure that the only wise thing was to tell everything; so she did exactly that, omitting only the state of Mark's nerves and the fact that Derek had become much more jumpy of late, and unpredictable. Warren Turnbull took notes, writing shorthand so swiftly that she found it hard to believe he would be able to read it back, but he didn't seem perturbed.

She reached the moment when she had felt the stranger's hands at her throat.

"Must have been bad," said Turnbull. "Did you catch a glimpse of the swine?"

"Well—"

"Must be accurate," he said brusquely. "You did or you didn't, you know."

That annoyed her, although she knew that the rebuke was half-deserved.

"I saw the man," she said, "but I didn't see his face. He wore something over it. I *did* see his eyes, but it was almost dark, and—"

"Dark clothes or light?"

"Dark—well, more dark than light."

"Tall, short, medium?"

"Rather short, I should say."

"Not bad at all," said Turnbull genially; "anyone who can keep her eyes open and wits about her while being strangled has got something!" He stood up. "Thanks, Miss Howard; I don't think I need worry you any more. There'll be a guard back and front, of course, and from now on you'll be followed wherever you go. Don't try and shake off our men, will you?"

That annoyed her, too.

"Why do you imagine I would try?"

He gave that broad, bold grin again; it was almost a jeer.

"The age of romance isn't dead yet, is it?"

When he had gone out, her cheeks were flaming and she felt hot with anger; she cooled very slowly. She had never been affected by anyone in the same way. The man as a man pushed what had happened into the background, she was obsessed by him and not by the attempt to murder her. It wasn't until she was back in bed, lying down, that she began to feel the shock of that. She started to tremble. She knew she wouldn't be able to sleep again, and got up and began to walk about. Now and again she looked at the window and the alley. If Warren Turnbull hadn't followed her, she would have been murdered. Could there have been any other result of the attack?

She would have been the fourth Beauty Queen to die.

*   *   *

Roger West kissed Janet lightly on the cheek, and then hurried along the garden path to his car. There, Martin was sitting at the wheel, giving the horn an occasional honk, and Richard was testing the springs, bouncing up and down on the seat next to the driver's, and obviously trying to bounce high enough to hit the roof with his head.

"That'll do, lunatics," Roger said. "Over, Scoop, I'm in a hurry."

Scoopy was already moving over.

"Mind *me!*" protested Richard.

"I didn't touch you."

"Oh, you did. Dad, he did. Tell him—"

"Settle your own quarrels, Fish," Roger said, and started off at a pace which told them—and the watching Janet—that he was thinking of nothing so commonplace as his family.

Janet smiled to herself, Richard sulked a bit, Martin sat quite still.

The boys jumped out at the end of a street near their school, and joined a throng of others.

Roger put on speed to the Yard.

He had had a telephone call from a Night Duty Superintendent, and was anxious to know much more than that sketchy report. It gave the facts but not the details, and told him that Turnbull had taken everything into his own hands and had not thought it worth while calling him, Roger. No other man of lower rank with whom Roger had ever worked would have done that, on a case of this kind. Two with whom he had worked for years, Sloan and Peel, had recently gone to Divisions, with promotions; he missed them at times of high pressure.

He parked the car and positively scurried to his room—and then pulled up short.

" 'Morning, Handsome," greeted Turnbull.

He was in Roger's chair again; at least he had the grace to stand up at once. Looking at him closely, Roger could see that his eyes were slightly bleary, although that was the only indication of tiredness. He seemed on top of the world as he tapped a broad forefinger onto a sheaf of papers.

"That's the report of the night's doings. Nothing much—no dabs or anything—it's all there."

"Thanks. I thought you'd be in bed—was told you'd reported just after six." It was now a few minutes after nine o'clock.

"I had forty winks upstairs," Turnbull said. "Thought I'd better bring you right up to date before getting some real shuteye. It could be quite a day! I think you'll find everything in there, but there are some things I ought to amplify." Turnbull took out a gold cigarette case and put a cigarette to his lips. In self-defense, Roger lit a Virginian. "These chaps Derek Talbot and Mark Osborn want plenty of watching. They're each ready to cut the other's throat."

"Over what?"

"Regina Howard. Mark Osborn took her to dinner at a cozy little spot near Paddington. Talbot must have known the restaurant; he turned up at a nearby pub soon afterward, got himself drunk, and then went in to fight Osborn. He lost."

"Sure about all this?" Roger asked.

"Yep." Turnbull didn't allow a moment's doubt. "Been dog-eat-dog for weeks. I've checked with a man at Pomerall's and another at Conway's. But Gina doesn't seem to favor either. She might have a slight bias toward Mark, but Derek's the boy with the little gray cells, so that makes it about even. I'll tell you something else."

"I'd like to know it," Roger said, dryly.

"The man who attacked Regina could have been Derek Talbot. If he crouched a bit, he'd fit in for size. Knew the district, too. If we'd been watching them for the past few weeks we might know a thing or two. As it is, I'm having both men checked; if they were out during the early hours it'll be worth knowing. Osborn delivered Talbot to his Mayfair flat about eleven o'clock, and stayed long enough to undress him and put him to bed. Then he drove off—that's as far as I've got, except that he was certainly home at a quarter-past five."

"How do you know that?"

"I telephoned him."

"And Talbot?"

"I telephoned him, too," Turnbull answered, "but I didn't get any answer. Mind you, Derek Talbot was drunk the way that leaves the worst possible hangovers, he might have had so many noises in his head that he couldn't tell a telephone bell from a fire alarm. Again, he might be one who sobers up fast." Suddenly, Turnbull yawned, but didn't apologize. "Who'd want to kill these Beauty Queens, Handsome?"

"That's what we're finding out," Roger said. "Thanks for all this. Now go and get some sleep, you'll probably be busy again tonight."

"Not a bad idea, at that." Turnbull yawned again. "Just a thought—Regina Howard's really something. She's the nearest thing to a certainty for that big prize. Takes after her mother, I've discovered—Mrs. H. was the sensation of the stage in

106

her youth. Had an accident, lost her beauty, found it again in daughter Gina. If someone has a favorite and wants to make sure the favorite wins, then all competition—"

Roger just raised a hand, sharply.

"Still too farfetched?" asked Turnbull, and shrugged his shoulders derisively. "Well, could be. But one murder in two wouldn't be committed if the motive wasn't farfetched. You'd have to have someone with a twisted mind for this, but not insane, mind you. Just a one-track mind."

"Like me," Roger said. "You're off duty."

"Okay, sergeant," Turnbull said, and strode out.

Roger waited until his footsteps faded along the passage, and then picked up the report. It was like the others from Turnbull—meticulous in detail, simply and effectively phrased. It was the kind of report that spelled accuracy, and was remarkable because a man who had been up all night had written it.

...the assailant turned right, into Beckington Way, which I know to lead to seven different streets. I did not follow, therefore, but returned to the house and telephoned the office, put out a call for the man with a description. I then questioned Miss Howard, who was in some emotional distress, which she kept well under control. Her main anxiety was for her mother, who is suffering from a disease of the heart, which...

Roger finished the report.

The harder one looked, the more apparent it became that the Beauty Queens were victims of a campaign of violence. Why? Just because they were Beauty Queens, or because someone with a warped mind thought that by killing them off he could secure the prize for a girl whom he favored?

It was a vague kind of premise, but had to be examined closely. The surviving Queens were important in two ways, now: one, because any one of them might be attacked; two, because any one of those who still survived might be the one whom a murderer favored—for whom he was killing.

The next thing was to decide how to handle the newspapers. Roger wanted to see Chatworth about that, particularly because of Conway's. Conway's would probably screech that the notoriety was costing them a fortune, but that wouldn't be true and their protest didn't matter. But did the Yard want the Press to play the murders up too much? And if they didn't, could it be stopped?

There were the three organizers to be questioned, too—Talbot, Osborn, and the older man, Dickerson. Once it was accepted that anyone with an interest in a Queen might be behind the murders, the net was spread very wide.

Roger sent instructions to the detective officers who were watching the three organizers, to make sure that all three were followed during the day, and proposed to question them in the evening. First, he meant to see Regina Howard. He wanted to check the story which she had told Turnbull, and he mustn't lose sight of the fact that Turnbull might be biased by a pretty face. Only "pretty" wasn't quite the word.

He made sure, by telephone, that the girl was at the fashion agency offices, and was about to leave his room when the telephone rang. It was the man who had been sent to watch Wilfrid Dickerson.

Dickerson was missing from his home.

Very soon they discovered that Dickerson's fingerprints had been on the roof and in the church of St. Cleo's.

12

A Man Named
Dickerson

The Yard and the Divisions swung into action.
They had a good man to hunt, a man photographed a hundred times in the Beauty Competitions, a smallish, lean fellow, rather diffident in
manner according to all who knew him, balding,
middle-aged, physically strong. People came forward quickly, almost tumbling over each other,
with stories of the strength which Wilfrid Dickerson had in his hands; especially in his hands. He
could tear a telephone directory across; he could
bend iron bars; he could break thick pieces of
wood. Allowing for all the exaggeration, Dickerson had the kind of hands a strangler might have.

Witnesses were eager to speak; no one appeared
to like Dickerson.

He had very short, imbedded nails, from child-
hood biting—from adolescence biting, perhaps.
The flesh grew out over the nails, and the picture
was of flat-tipped fingers very smooth and fleshy—

the kind of fingers Turnbull had theorized for the murderer of Betty Gelibrand.

A wiry, well-preserved, physically fit man of early middle age, then, with a little nervous cough, a hoarse voice, pale features, rather small and sharp, and hooded blue eyes. Item by item the picture grew and was passed on to waiting police stations, and the call spread from London and the Home Counties to the Midlands, the West, and the North—west to Eire, then across the Channel to France and Belgium, across the North Sea to Holland and Scandinavia.

And the Press had to come in.

They published pictures of Dickerson and the old and trusty caption: "The man whom the police are anxious to interview in connection with the murder of Rose Alderson." Betty Gelibrand and Hilda Shaw weren't mentioned, because the Press and the public already believed that their killer had been found. Or some of the Press did. The *Globe*'s midday edition carried headlines:

HUNT FOR BEAUTY QUEENS' KILLER
THREE STRANGLED

It burst on London, took possession of the front pages, caught the public imagination. It became a subject for causal conversation or hushed talk in train and bus, home and shop. *"Isn't it terrible?"* Pictures of the three dead girls appeared in the evening edition of the *Globe*—and also pictures of the living Queens; Regina Howard among them.

Roger hadn't interviewed Regina yet.

He saw Mark Osborn, whose story seemed straightforward, who agreed that he was scared—for Regina. Turnbull was right again, Mark Osborn was certainly in love with the girl. Roger left Derek Talbot until the evening, because Talbot hadn't gone to his office until late, and had then rushed off on some urgent Competition job.

There were the directors of Conway's, two pompous, one practical; they all agreed that it couldn't be helped, pooh-poohed the suggestion that Dickerson, one of their employees, could be involved, promised all the help they could give, and gave the police a free hand at Bennis Place. Meanwhile, the Competition could be suspended if necessary. And:

"Go where you like, do what you like, hrrmph! If there is a killer of these girls, find him." That was the usual maddeningly condescending attitude of certain kinds of big businessmen. "We don't want any more of this kind of publicity. Not doing us any good."

"I'd like to see all the forms of publicity used for the Competition," Roger said, woodenly.

It was extensive, but didn't help him much. Yet he left with much respect for Conway's publicity experts. He learned, for instance, how many tens of thousands of show cards, with pictures of the Queens, had been distributed—and were now being withdrawn.

"Can't use them when a gel's dead," the managing director said. "Costing a small fortune, too. And trade's falling. Do everything, won't you?"

Roger said evenly: "I certainly want to stop the killer from killing again."

"Oh, yes, hrrmph, of course."

"How long has Dickerson been with you?" Roger asked.

"Donkey's years," the managing director said. "Long before I joined the corporation. In fact, he's a fixture. Was in a small way of business himself, and came in with us. Soap in his blood, you might say. Most loyal, steady servant. I can't believe..."

Roger let him finish.

At last a fairly complete picture of Dickerson was formed. They had his history, which wasn't remarkable. He was a widower, had been widowed for fifteen years, had no children, his hobby was collecting fashion plates, he had a magnificent collection going back to the sixteenth century. He was just a little "odd." He had a small flat in Bloomsbury, no one knew where he went when he went out, but he was often out in the evening.

"Get on to every angle," Roger ordered; "don't let anything slip."

He had been at the desk most of the day, co-ordinating, thinking, streamlining, bursting to go out and to question Talbot and the girl, but unable to get away. Then there came the late-afternoon lull. Quickly, he put on his coat and straightened his collar and tie and drove to Regina Howard's place, taking matter-of-fact Sergeant Dalby with him.

Derek Talbot was at Regina's flat.

Roger sensed the tough streak in Talbot within a few seconds of greeting. This man would deceive a lot of people. Overlong hair, a slight perfume, exquisite clothes, beautifully kept nails coated with a plain varnish, delicate skin—but underneath it all, something that was very close to steel.

113

He was in the small living room, with Regina. Mrs. Howard wasn't there.

Regina looked a tired beauty.

"Oh, not *another*," she said, when Roger introduced himself, and Talbot gave an approving, sardonic smile. Then she closed her eyes, and when she spoke again it was rather more calmly. "I'm sorry, Chief Inspector, but it's been nothing but police and newspapermen all day, first here, then the office, now here again. And I'm afraid—"

She broke off.

"Of what, Miss Howard?" Roger was very matter of fact, and Talbot's lips curved in something not far from a sneer.

"I don't want my mother to be worried," Regina said firmly. "She knows that something's wrong, but doesn't yet know what it is. She's with friends along the street just now. I don't know whether it's any use, but I'd like to keep it from her."

Roger was still flat-voiced.

"Why?"

"My dear man," Talbot began, superciliously.

"Derek, please." Regina wouldn't let him finish. "She's just not well. I know the shock wouldn't kill her, but it might make her worse. And if she thought that I might be in danger, I don't know what she'd do."

"Do you seriously think you can keep this from her?"

"Of course she can, police permitting," Talbot put in.

The girl looked at him, saying silently: *"Please, Derek."*

"We won't stop you trying," Roger said briskly. "Now, Miss Howard, I'd like to ask you a few questions in private, please." He waited until Talbot had gone out of the room, showing great reluctance, and Dalby was ready with his pencil and notebook. "How well did you know Wilfrid Dickerson?"

"I knew him—quite well," Regina said.

"How long have you known him?"

"For about ten years."

"As long as that?" The answer startled Roger. "You didn't first meet him through the Competition, then?"

"Oh, no," said Regina. "No, he was a friend of my father, and met Mother again about ten years ago. He was often a visitor here. It was he who first introduced me to Mr. Talbot and Mr. Osborn. He was most anxious for me to enter the Competition, too."

"Why?" Roger asked flatly.

Her answer seemed quite frank.

"He knows that I can't really afford to live at home—in fact, he helped me to get the office job I have now—but he would like me to be free to help Mother. He—he's very fond of her."

Roger let it go at that for the time being.

"Did everyone connected with the firm know that you were friendly with the Competition officials?"

"There's no reason why they shouldn't," Regina answered sharply. "The judges are quite independent." She changed the subject abruptly. "I've seen the newspapers, but to think that Wilf Dickerson would attack me—" She gave a funny little laugh. "Even if it were possible that he would attack the others, I just can't believe he would harm me."

"Why not?"

115

"He's been such a good friend."

"Affectionately?"

"I don't quite understand you."

"It's become pretty clear that Mr. Talbot and Mr. Osborn are affectionately disposed," Roger said, and smiled faintly. "Was Mr. Dickerson a third string?"

Something in the way he said that made her laugh unexpectedly.

"Gracious, no!"

"Sure?"

"I don't believe—" began Regina, and then stopped. She closed her eyes again, and then sat down rather heavily. "Oh, I can't be sure of anything," she said helplessly. "But I don't think that Wilfrid thought of me as anything but—" She opened her eyes at their lovely widest and brightest. "This sounds so hackneyed, but you'll know what I mean. I think he had a *paternal* interest only."

"But you can't be sure."

"How can I be?"

She seemed like an honest witness, and that was important. She also seemed genuinely worried. Roger switched the subject to the other two men. Obviously she wasn't happy about their relationship. She was uneasy about what had happened at the restaurant, tried to make light of it, but admitted that if it hadn't been for Mark Osborn's swift action, it would have been very unpleasant.

"Miss Howard," Roger said with a sudden switch, "did you get the impression that Mr. Dickerson is abnormally interested in you winning the big prize in the finals?"

"He—he would like me to."

"Is he very keen?"

"He—" she hesitated.

"Surely you can answer this one," Roger urged. "I don't want to keep you too long. Your mother may return, and she'll wonder what this is about."

"Yes," Regina said quietly. "Wilfrid seemed to have set his heart on it. I wanted"—she gave an odd little laugh—"I wanted to withdraw."

"Why?"

"Well, I'd hate to think favoritism—I mean, I'd hate to think that anyone could put down any success I had to favoritism." She colored up. "As I've said, it's fair enough."

"No film ambitions?" Roger asked, and that seemed to help her.

"And I'm not stage-struck, either!"

Roger grinned.

"It's nice to know we understand each other. What about the others—Mr. Osborn and Mr. Talbot? Were they anxious for you to win?"

"Well—I suppose so."

"One more than the other?"

"I can't see why you're asking all these questions," Regina's voice sharpened again. "What's the point of it? If someone were trying to kill all the others off so as to give—to give me a clear run—" She broke off, caught her breath, and then cried, "No, it's too fantastic!"

"I hope it is," Roger said. "We—"

"But even if it were true, and it can't be true," Regina cried almost wildly, "why did they attack me? Does that make any sense?"

"Not yet," Roger conceded, "but we may find some in it yet. Did—perhaps I should say does—

either Mr. Talbot or Mr. Osborn want you to win more than the other?"

"I suppose I'll have to tell you." Regina gave way reluctantly. "Mark doesn't care very much, but Derek's very keen. It still doesn't make any sense. I—"

She broke off.

There was a sound at the front door, and she moved toward it quickly, her grace and her speed alike surprising Roger. He didn't try to stop her, but watched. The door had opened to admit a small, thin woman in a gray skirt, who came in very slowly. Roger saw the astonishing beauty of one side of her face; and the mask of the other.

"Mother!" cried Regina.

"It's all right, my dear," Mrs. Howard said, and Roger felt the tension in her voice. "I shall be all right when I've got over the shock. I've seen the *Evening Globe*, and your picture's in it. And—and Wilfrid's."

She swayed; if Regina hadn't been there, she would have fallen.

13

Fear

Derek Talbot stood in the doorway, head on one side, half-sneering. The impression of steely strength was very strong, so was the evidence of moral courage; yet behind the smile, the suaveness, and the hinted insults, there was something else.

Was it fear?

Regina was in the bedroom with her mother.

"It must be nice being a policeman," Talbot said. "Tearing the private lives of other people into little pieces. Don't you get fun?"

"When we start tearing up the private lives of other people, we do it because we have to, not because we like it," Roger said. "But we do it. You might think it worth reflection that we didn't talk to Mrs. Howard—the Press and neighbors did that."

"Remote control," gibed Talbot.

He looked, spoke, and acted as if he wanted to antagonize Roger; and it would be easy to get tough. But not wise. There was one real enemy, the murderer, and whether they liked it or not, all the rest could be used to help to find out who it was. So Roger said mildly, "Please yourself, we do all we can. How well do you know Dickerson?"

"Our Wilf? Very well. He is the kind of man who won't kill a fly or tread on an ant if he can help it. The dull but kindly type. Generous, too. Just so that you won't jump for joy when you discover it, he's lent me seven hundred and thirteen pounds ten shillings during the past eighteen months or so, so if I bumped him off I wouldn't have to pay it back, would I? It's just between the two of us."

So Talbot was hard up.

"Have you noticed anything particular about his attitude to the Competition winners?"

"Yes," said Talbot promptly. "Avuncular, not to say paternal solicitude. Marvelous chap, our Wilf —either nerves of steel or blood like soap and water. He can weave around these pretties, and believe me they are pretties, and take measurements, size 'em up when—my goodness, that big chap who calls himself a Detective Inspector would cause a riot! He'd have the brazenest hussy screeching for a new age of chivalry. But Wilf is the perfect impersonal measure-upper. Better than another woman, because the girls would probably think she was being jealous, and curbing the curves. You could rely on our Wilf for both immaculate honesty and behavior. He would point a finger at a beauteous bosom and ask if it were enhanced by artificial aid with a voice as dry as cornflakes without milk. And did he spot 'em! Come to think," added Talbot, screwing up his nose, "he was unerring. Never a falsy passed the eagle eye of Father Wilf."

He stopped, took out a cigarette case, and un-bent far enough to offer it.

"Virginian," he said. "I find Turkish offensive, al-though you wouldn't think so to look at me, would you?"

In the right mood, he could be likable; and he seemed to dislike Turnbull, making sure that all his digs went home.

"Thanks," Roger said. They lit up. "Does Dicker-son show any favoritism toward any one of the competitors?"

"Yes."

"Who?"

"Regina, our Regina."

"Are you sure?"

"He loves her as a daughter. Undoubtedly he wishes she was, for he loves her mother. One day in his cups, and that is rare, he told me that he'd been a rejected suitor of Mrs. Howard when she was at her beautiful best. But, being Wilf, he ad-mitted that the best man won her. As Mrs. Howard was not for him, he fusses over Regina like the Sultan's harem mistress of the days of good King Neb. His eyes and behavior are coldly fishlike to-ward every other charmer, but not toward Regina. I hope," went on Talbot, very deliberately, "that you understand that I am doing my best to be hon-est. Your natural charm has overcome my dislike of policemen, especially copper-headed cops."

Roger grinned suddenly, broad, a man-to-man grin.

"You've a rod in pickle for Turnbull, haven't you?"

"I have. I don't like his manner. He was at the office this afternoon, and I did not like the way he talked to Regina. In case there is the slightest doubt in your mind, I am devoted to Regina. I wish to marry her. I am a peculiar person, no doubt, and absurdly jealous. As you have doubtless learned after my exhibition of appalling bad manners and weak-mindedness last night. You see what love will do to a man. Not only did I dislike the way in which your Mr. Turnbull talked to my Miss Regina," went on Talbot, very gently, "but I greatly resented the way he looked at her. That isn't an indictable offense, but it might lead to one. Because," went on Talbot in the same soft tone, "I shall undoubtedly assault him if he looks at Regina in the same lascivious way again. Have I made myself clear?"

Roger said easily, "You're reading too much into it."

"You have been warned."

"Thanks. We were talking about Dickerson. Are you sure that he showed no favoritism toward anyone else?"

"As sure as I am that he wouldn't attack Regina," Talbot said.

Roger learned nothing else from him; nothing else from Regina Howard. He gathered that Mrs. Howard was all right, now, and lying down; her chief trouble was an obscure disease of the heart, Talbot inferred, which might catch up on her at any time. No one put it into words, but Mrs. Howard was obviously living precipitously between life and death. She'd had one bad shock; she might succumb to another. That would explain much of Regina's anxieties, and also made it tough.

Roger left, with a feeling of liking for Derek Talbot, uneasy about Turnbull—who hadn't reported for duty, but had gone straight to Conway's offices. Turnbull was going to come a cropper before long. It was easy to understand what Talbot meant, too; the way Turnbull looked at women was likely to cause a lot of trouble.

You couldn't talk to a man about the way he looked.

The story of Dickerson's abortive love for Mrs. Howard was a factor to be remembered.

Roger went to Mark Osborn's service flat, in St. John's Wood. Osborn was in, and said much the same as Talbot had about Dickerson. He showed his anxiety more clearly, and there was the story of his fears the night before when Regina had talked to him. There was also the way he had attacked Talbot, and squeezed out of an awkward situation; the man of action who didn't like waiting, didn't like suspense. There was uneasiness in his gray eyes.

He seemed to be answering frankly.

When Roger had finished, Osborn said in an edgy voice, "Now let me ask you a few questions. Do you know who's behind all this?"

"Not yet."

"Do you seriously think it's Wilf Dickerson?"

"When we've had a chance to talk to him, I'll know more about that."

"I can't understand what's happened to him," Osborn muttered; then squared his shoulders, hesitated, and burst out, "Do you think Regina's in danger?" He gripped Roger's arm tightly. "Are you looking after her properly?"

"We'll look after her."

"You'd better," Osborn said abruptly. "If you let anything happen to Regina—" He broke off. "And what about the others?" His voice became hard and aggressive. "I mean the other Queens. What about them?"

"We're looking after them, too," Roger assured him.

He left, convinced that fear lay deep in Osborn's mind. It was laying its clammy hand on everyone. Why? Were there things in the past life of the two men which they didn't want uncovered? What had Talbot been getting at when he had talked about breaking up private lives? Was he fearful of what the police might find about him?

The Yard was probing deeply into his past; Osborn's; Dickerson's; Regina Howard's and her mother's—and the Divisions were looking after the other three surviving Queens. When one thought of it like that, and realized that only four out of seven winners were alive, it hurt like the kick of a horse. There were the other district winners to come—if Conway's went on with the show. If circumstances made them suspend the heats it would be a heavy blow to the Yard's prestige.

Roger put that worry out of his mind, and concentrated on Turnbull. Turnbull was simply keeping up with his job. Wasn't he? If a man could be blamed for working when he was officially off duty and when he was tired, then he, Roger, would have been thrown out of the Force years ago.

He went back to the Yard, but Turnbull wasn't there. He'd left a message in a sealed envelope, safe from prying eyes. Roger opened it.

Turnbull had discovered that Dickerson was an old suitor of Mrs. Howard; that he had worked his way back into her life after the accident in which her husband was killed. He'd found out that Dickerson was always helping Regina, and believed that was to win favor with the older woman.

Yes, Turnbull was good.

It was a reporter on the *Globe* who told Roger—quite casually and without knowing that it was news—that Turnbull and Regina Howard had lunch together that day.

There were also plenty of reports from the Division; and one word seemed to run through them all, the ugly word—fear.

The other three Queens were undoubtedly badly frightened, and not without cause. The headlines of the newspapers screeched at them; three Queens were dead, savagely murdered—*who goes next?* ran the refrain. The Press could feed the thirst of a nation for sensation only at the cost of hurting a few—and they hurt and frightened this trio badly. Headlines spared them nothing:

> BEAUTY QUEENS IN DANGER
> BEAUTY QUEEN NUMBER 5 WALKS IN FEAR
> WILL BEAUTY QUEEN KILLER STRIKE AGAIN?
> SCOTLAND YARD BEWILDERED

So it went on; with the photographs of the girls and of Dickerson, and the hunt for Dickerson working up to a shrieking crescendo. The Yard had started it, the newspapers meant to keep it going at high pitch. The *Globe* offered a reward of £500. The *Record* gratuitously offered protection to each of the surviving Queens, without saying that each reporter-protector hoped to get a firsthand story of an attack. There was no rest from all this for three days—but there were no more attacks.

Unless something else happened, the hullaballoo would die down, and then danger would come again.

There was no new slant.

Dickerson wasn't found.

Roger and Turnbull sifted the thousands of reports that came in about people who "looked" like Dickerson from police stations and the public all over the country. Several false alarms came from the ports, too.

A variety of facts was gradually established.

Derek Talbot was in debt to everyone, from his tailor to his close friends. He had a salary of fifteen hundred a year, and spent money freely at the rate of nearly three thousand. So he was desperately hard up, and money mattered to him. Until a few months ago, he had spent most of his money on the gay life, his girl friends had been many and expensive. He had dropped these since he had fallen in love with Regina. There was no doubt at all; she obsessed him. Few days passed when he didn't send her flowers, chocolates, or expensive gifts.

Mark Osborn wasn't exactly wealthy, but was comfortably off. He lived on a thousand a year, and was able to save plenty. He had no known vices, no steady girl friends; he played cricket, tennis, and golf, and was no mean swimmer. Everything pointed to his feeling as great a love for Regina as Talbot.

Dickerson was comfortably off; there was no apparent reason why he should have lent Talbot so much money, and none why he shouldn't.

More details were turned up about his association with the Howard family. Turnbull discovered an old friend of Dickerson's who swore that when

Mrs. Howard had married, Dickerson had been in desperate emotional straits. He had not seen her for many years, but had been among the first to offer practical sympathy after the accident.

Mrs. Howard hadn't much money, and had been grateful for his friendship and the help he was always ready to give to Regina.

It was Regina to whom Dickerson seemed devoted now.

Much revolved around Regina. . . .

But there were the other Queens.

"Looks to me as if Dickerson or the killer's having a rest," Turnbull said on the evening of the fourth day after the hunt had started for Dickerson. "We've probably scared him off, anyhow. With each of the Queens watched night and day, he hasn't much chance of having another crack at 'em. May find it will all quieten down a bit now, Handsome."

"We've still a murderer on our hands."

"We'll find him," Turnbull said confidently. "There's one Queen no one will do any harm to, I'll see to that."

By his silence, Roger implied that he knew that Turnbull had seen Regina Howard several times.

"Don't you approve?" Turnbull growled, and when Roger didn't answer, changed the subject abruptly. "Your kids all right?"

"Fine, thanks."

"Bet they wonder if they're ever going to see you again," Turnbull said. "That's the trouble with night work and you married chaps. Ought to be single, like me. There's a time and a place for everything." He gave his big, wolfish grin, but it soon faded. "Tell you a thing that's been on my mind."

"Go ahead," Roger said.

"Okay. Three beauties have been strangled. Then the devil had a go at Gina Howard, and we stopped him. If he wants to make a clean sweep, will he stick to strangling? In his place, I wouldn't. I'd try something else, something unexpected. Say, poison."

Roger said evenly, "Have you any reason to suspect poison?"

"No, I'm guessing. But I can tell you that all the Queens get a monthly box of chocolates, as part of their prize. They're sent from Conway's. Easy way, wouldn't it be?"

"Yes," Roger argeed reluctantly. "Too easy."

Turnbull had worried him; but it might be nothing more than the probing of a restless mind. There were too many things unknown. Where Dickerson was and why he'd run off. Why Millsom, if he hadn't killed Betty Gelibrand, had run away —and hidden. How Dickerson had known where to find him.

Turnbull was going through some reports, Roger writing, when the telephone bell rang, and a moment later, for the first time for weeks, he put the Queen's murder out of his mind. For this was Janet, a scared Janet.

"Roger, can you come home? It's Richard—in fact it's both of them, but Richard's worse. He's in agony, and I'm so scared."

Roger felt the cold clutch of fear which came whenever danger threatened at home. And Turnbull's talk of poison suddenly took on a new, dread meaning.

"I'll be over at once," he said. "Got the doctor?"

"Oh, yes, he's with him now. First Richard was

sick, then Scoop, but Scoop didn't make much fuss. Richard—Oh! Did you hear *that?*"

The world had become a place of fear in a different way, for Roger had heard "that": a scream of pain from Richard.

"Twenty minutes," he said, and rang off.

"You forget everything, Handsome," Turnbull said swiftly. "I'll fix things here. I'll tell the A.C., too. Just scramble."

Roger said, "Thanks."

He hurried out of the office. Everyone who could get in his way did so. Men who wanted to stay and have a chat gaped when he passed with a curt word. The great Chatworth himself was actually getting out of his car, and waved; and Roger shouted, "Sorry, sir, see Turnbull!"

He was at the wheel and on the way, taking the fast Embankment Road, within ten minutes of getting the message. But a swarm of traffic coming off Lambeth Bridge snarled him, and it was nearly half an hour before he reached Bell Street. There the fear became starker, became something near horror, for an ambulance stood outside the house.

The front door was open.

Neighbors were watching.

Roger went in and called: "Janet!" and then heard voices upstairs and rushed up them three at a time.

Janet and the doctor, gray-haired, leathery-cheeked, blue-eyed Dr. James, were in the bathroom. An ambulance man and a nurse were in the boys' bedroom.

Janet hadn't a spot of color in her cheeks.

"Take it easy, Mr. West," Dr. James said. "It isn't as bad as it might be, but your young men have been eating something that doesn't agree with them. I'd rather have them in hospital under observation. Yes, Mrs. West, you can go and see they're well looked after—of course you can go in the ambulance." Janet squeezed Roger's hand and hurried out, and Roger turned to follow, but the doctor said, "Half a minute, Mr. West."

Roger turned, sharply.

"I don't want to worry your wife too much," Dr. James said, "but I want the stomach contents analyzed quickly. We've had a lot of serious food-poisoning epidemics. Don't want to take any chances."

"I'll fix the analysis," Roger promised. He felt dreadful.

14

Poison Chocolates

There was a bowl in the bedroom, a stomach pump, the invariable sick-room smell. Dr. James, looking like an ogre, nodded confirmation of what he had said.

"They've eaten a lot of chocolates tonight—Richard especially—and I suppose it could have been in that. Anyhow, I've got the stomach contents. Don't *want* to scare you, but the quicker you get on to a thing like this the better."

"Yes," Roger said. He had telephoned for a squad car, and heard it arrive. He took the bowl downstairs and gave it to the sergeant-driver, with precise instructions. Then he went back upstairs. His head ached, he couldn't think clearly; whenever a crisis of this kind came he realized how taut his nerves were. "Thanks. Mind if I have a look at the boys?"

"Richard's dopey, Martin's not too bad," the doctor said.

Scoopy looked wan; and Richard looked like death. Janet, the worst shock over, was competent, with a lot to do, night clothes to get ready, toilet bags to pack. Life had changed in a matter of hours.

The boys were carried down to the ambulance, as neighbors clucked in sympathy.

And Janet talked all the time. . . .

"They were perfectly all right when they got home, but they were late, it was nearly seven. I scolded them, they mustn't stay late unless I know about it, and then I said that they must go to bed early, as punishment. So I got their supper, and Scoop didn't want much. That was unbelievable! Richard wouldn't touch a thing, either. Apparently they'd been eating a lot of chocolate, and some sandwiches one of the other boys gave them. I think Richard spent all his pocket money on chocolates, I told you not to give him so much this week, you never will do what I tell you!"

"Did they say anything about it?"

"No."

"Where are Richard's clothes?" Roger asked, and Janet picked up Richard's flannel trousers. Coins jingled in the pocket. Roger slid his fingers inside and drew out a two-shilling piece, two sixpences, and some coppers. "I gave him four shillings yesterday," he said, "because I owed him two, so he's spent sixpence at the most."

"Well, he got the chocolate from *some*where," Janet cried. Then her eyes filled with tears. "Darling, I'm sorry if I'm being beastly, but it was such a shock. I think I will go in the ambulance. Unless you—"

"You go," Roger said quickly. "I'll try to find out what they did eat. There may be other kids suffering from it, too. Food poisoning, probably."

"Not from chocolate!"

"We don't know that it was in the chocolate." Roger walked with her to the door, and watched her get in beside the boys. Martin's eyes flickered, and Roger said, "What did you eat, Scoop?"

The boy just looked at him, dazedly.

"Roger, don't!" whispered Janet.

"Jan, listen. Make him tell you what they've eaten. It won't do Scoopy any harm, and it might be very important. Try to find out."

"We must be off now, sir," an ambulance man said.

"Yes. Sorry. Jan, don't forget." Roger moved away, Janet and the boys were shut away from him. He went to the house. Two constables had come up, and asked if they could help; so did four neighbors. "No, thanks," Roger said to them all, and went in and closed the door firmly.

He was alone.

He was at a taut stretch, and if anything went wrong with the boys he would crack. He knew it; parentage had its own secret terrors.

He fought the near ones off.

There were things which needed doing; he had to clear his mind of the emotions which the illness of the boys created; had to be dispassionate, had to study this as a policeman. The boys were suffering from poisoning, and they couldn't have swallowed it more than three hours or so ago. So he had to trace every movement they'd made in the past four hours, say.

He'd need Divisional help.

He called the Chelsea Division, talked to the Superintendent in charge, knew that every man available there would be on the job. It was still daylight. He poured himself a drink, then had a snack in the kitchen, and soon heard a car draw up. He went to the front door.

Turnbull was striding up the garden path.

"Hallo, Handsome. How're those kids of yours?" He sounded as if he was really anxious to know; and he looked it.

"Could be worse, I'm told."

"Oh, good! They here?"

"Hospital."

"Phee-oooh! Anxious times for the little woman," Turnbull said. "Sure they're all right? Been eating too much? Between you and me, I'd do a lot for that elder kid of yours, young Scoop; first time I've ever really wished I was married. Young Big Ears is quite a lad, too. Sure they're all right?"

"They won't die. They simply swallowed some poison."

Turnbull just echoed, "Poison." In a queer way, his reaction to that news was more affecting than anything he had said earlier. He looked genuinely shocked, and gave the impression that he was really interested in the boys.

The two Yard men stared at each other, without speaking, until Roger said, "Let's have a drink— whisky or beer?"

"Whisky, thanks."

They sipped whiskies and soda.

"But hell, how'd they get hold of it? They're not infants who'd swallow anything they came across, some weed-killer say. Say, Handsome, no one would—"

He didn't finish.

"Poison them," Roger said. "I've been telling myself that's crazy, too."

As he spoke, a queer possibility entered his head; he hadn't given it a moment's thought before. To think that anyone deliberately set out to poison the boys was crazy—fantastic—farfetched beyond all words. Like the Beauty Queen killer's motive. Two things happened together, equally improbable, equally true.

"But damn it all—" Turnbull wasn't really himself, was bewildered; a refreshingly human manifestation.

"Don't like it," Roger said. "Half a mo'." He pushed past Turnbull and picked up the telephone. "I'm ringing the Yard," he said as he dialed. Then: "Chief Inspectors' room, please." He looked at the other man. "We'll play your hunch."

Turnbull was puffing Turkish tobacco furiously. Roger wrinkled his nose.

"Hallo, Gibby, West here....Have all the Queens checked in a hurry, will you? There's an outside chance that someone will try to feed them poison....Yes, I'll hold on." He kept the receiver at his ear and waved smoke away with his free hand. "Why don't you stop smoking that foul stuff?"

"What's Gibson want you to hold on for?"

"There's a message in for me."

"It's a hell of a hunch. Could be, though—poison your kids, poison the Queens. A new form of attack. Look, Handsome—"

"Quiet!...Yes, Gibby....Sure?" Roger's voice rose. "Oh, well, get the rest done at the double, will you? Yes, full statements from them all, make sure they don't eat any of the damned stuff....Thanks, old chap."

He rang off.

Turnbull was looking very pale; his eyes were

glittering, and the cigarette was stubbed out in an ashtray.

"Alice Harvey's been taken to hospital with suspected arsenical poisoning, after eating chocolates sent through the post," Roger said with great deliberation.

"My God!" gasped Turnbull; and added with hardly a pause, "I'm going to see Regina."

He turned and raced out of the room.

Everything was in hand, there was no point in staying—except that Janet might come back, or might telephone. Roger moved to the hall and then into the front garden. Turnbull was already in his car, the engine roaring; he didn't look round.

A neighbor appeared on her porch. "Is there anything I can do, Roger?"

"Nellie, be a dear and sit-in in case Janet calls," Roger said. "Or have her calls transferred to you—fix something, won't you?"

"Of course."

"Thanks." Roger smiled his thanks, hurried to the car, and started off three minutes after Turnbull. Now he had time to think of the effect of the news on the big man, and the way he had gasped: "I'm going to see Regina." Not "Regina Howard," but a burning, personal "Regina."

Regina was a key, too; and Gibson would see that the other Queens were warned. It was better to go to the Howards' flat than anywhere else.

Roger drove fast....

Two cars were outside Regina's place, the street door was open, every light was on. Roger heard Turnbull's voice, and an ominous, "What do you think, Doctor?" And after a pause, while a woman answered and Roger thought that Regina was the victim, Regina herself said, "Oh, thank goodness."

Roger tapped at the door. Turnbull opened it, and spoke before Roger could ask a question. Regina, looking huge-eyed, tired but so very lovely, was sitting down in an easychair. Another woman, presumably the doctor, was in the living room.

"Regina's all right, but her mother ate some chocolates which came by post this morning," Turnbull said. "Got the ruddy things, too." He thumped on a box which stood on the table, then moved to Regina and squeezed her arm. "Wrapping paper's salvaged, and it's smothered with prints." He gripped Roger's arm next, and shepherded him out of the room, much as a wise old counselor would draw an inexperienced youth to one side. "Let's go straight to Derek Talbot," he said, "he's always sending her chocolates. Or I will —you have the chocolates and the paper tested. If Talbot hasn't taken a run-out powder—"

"Take these things to the Yard, have them checked, and telephone me at Talbot's flat," Roger said, brusquely. "I'll telephone Osborn from here and have him meet me. Then I'll see Talbot."

Turnbull hated it, but said stonily, "You're the boss."

"Both men hate you guts," Roger said. "It's a bad thing to make people hate you like that. They might lie to hide something, and they might lie to make a fool of you. Get a move on, Warren!"

It was the first time he had used "Warren." Turnbull picked it up in a flash.

"Oke," he said, and hurried out.

Roger didn't wait for him to drive off, but turned

to the telephone, in the corner of the small hall. Regina Howard and the woman doctor were still talking. He didn't try to hear what they said, but dialed the Yard again. He made sure that both Talbot and Osborn were being watched, and that reports had come in recently.

"Double the watch on each man," he said.

"Right, sir. By the way, the laboratory's wanting you to ring them."

This would be the analyst's report about the boys.

"Thanks. Put me through," Roger said stonily.

He didn't have long to wait. He listened for ten seconds and then began to feel ridiculously weak. The report made one thing clear; there was no arsenic trouble with the boys, simply a form of ptomaine poisoning. There was a message from the hospital, too; three other children from the Bell Street neighborhood were down with food poisoning.

He wiped his forehead when he rang off.

Then he rang the hospital. Dr. James was there, had the same story to tell, and was reassuring. Scoopy was right out of the wood, Richard would be poorly for a few days; that was the worst.

It was easy to relax, now; to laugh at fears. Roger didn't laugh or relax for long, but dialed Osborn's number. The double guard should be in position.

Osborn answered....

"Oh, all right," he said, "I'll see you at Derek Talbot's flat. 'By."

He rang off.

Now Osborn could get in touch with Talbot; or

run away as Dickerson seemed to have; or simply do what he was told.

Roger was in the street where Talbot lived ten minutes later. He saw Osborn arrive, in the gathering gloom. Lights were on at Talbot's flat, and, a few moments later, Roger was assured by the portly, reassuring Sergeant Dalby, "They're both inside now, sir."

"Good," Roger said. "Thanks."

He hurried to the house. It was quite small, off one of London's squares, only ten minutes' walk from Medley's offices. Talbot lived on the top floor. Roger rang the bell, but there was no immediate response. He rang again. Nothing happened—but he heard unexpected sounds, a thumping and a thudding. Then, quite suddenly, glass splintered, he heard it crack, then heard it tinkle against the pavement. A few slivers actually fell on his hat.

The Yard man came running.

"They'll kill each other!" he exclaimed. "Look up there, sir!"

Roger backed away from the front door.

Up at the window of Talbot's flat, the two men could be seen in the light which streamed through the broken window. Talbot was leaning backward out of the window, and Osborn seemed to have his hands round Talbot's throat.

"Get that door down," Roger rapped.

15

The Rivals

The door had a glass panel, and the Yard man a quick mind. He smashed the glass with his elbow and put his hand inside, and Roger went in and up the stairs as swiftly as he had gone to the bedroom at home. Someone appeared at the first-floor landing, a gray-haired man who was staring at the ceiling. There were dull sounds from there now, but the thudding had stopped.

"Do you know—what's happening?"

"Don't worry," Roger said. He reached the next landing; Talbot's. This door had wooden panels. He put his shoulder to it and pushed with all his strength, but it didn't open. The Yard man joined him, and neither said a word, just drew back, then lunged; the door creaked. " 'Gain," grunted Roger. "On three. One—two—"

They launched the weight of nearly thirty stone against the door, and the lock couldn't stand it. The door yielded, but didn't fly open; precious seconds passed as they battered at it. Roger's mind carried the picture of Talbot leaning out of the window, almost helpless, and he could imagine what would happen to Talbot if he fell. Or what would happen if Osborn kept up that pressure.

The room doors were open.

Glass crashed, the floor shook, a man began to swear vilely. So there were two of them, still in there. Roger reached the room. The window was wide open and the curtains billowing, but the men weren't near it. Talbot was in a corner, with a hockey stick in his hands, raised for attack. Osborn was crouching just in front of him, hands empty, crooked, breathing hissingly.

Talbot's hair was hanging in front of his eyes, but didn't hide one eye, which was badly bruised. His lips were bleeding, too, and his tie had been wrenched to one side, his collar gaped. He held the stick with both hands, very tight and tense, expecting Osborn to spring at him, ready to smash it down.

"All right," Roger said, "that's plenty."

But he was wary.

Osborn started, glanced round—and then, sensing that Talbot would relax, leaped forward. And Talbot had turned to look at Roger. Too late, he brought the stick down. It hardly touched Osborn, who smashed at Talbot's chin and sent him rocketing against the wall.

Roger reached Osborn and hooked his legs from under him. As he crashed and the floor and the walls shook, Roger bent down and clipped him under the jaw. The blow didn't knock him out, but it dazed him.

"Make sure he doesn't do more murder," Roger said to Dalby, who had taken all this with complete calm.

"I'll watch him, sir."

Roger said, "Relax, Talbot," and then hurried out of the room. He wasn't surprised that the gray-haired man and two women were coming up the stairs. "It's all right," he reassured them, "I'm from Scotland Yard." He flashed his card as the gray-haired man reached the landing. "No need to worry."

He closed the door as well as he could, then turned back to the room. He was never likely to find Talbot in a readier mood for saying what he thought of Osborn.

Talbot, standing up, was running a comb through his hair. Even now, he was able to look at Roger with a faintly mocking smile.

"Mind if I repair the ravages?"

"Better come into the bathroom," Roger said. "Watch Osborn closely, Dalby," he added to the Yard man, and went off with Talbot. Talbot swayed, and grabbed the bathroom door for support. Roger helped him in, sat him on the bathroom stool and ran cold water in the hand basin. "It's spoiled your schoolgirl complexion," he said. "What was all that about?"

"The rivals," said Talbot.

"What set it off?"

"Being distressingly honest by nature, I suppose I must confess that I did. But it was bound to happen sooner or later, don't you think?"

"I thought the days of fighting over a girl were finished," Roger said, "but I'm prepared to believe in the return of the primitives. Did you know I sent him to see you?"

"No. Unkind."

"I wanted to talk to you both together. How did this shindy start?"

"Mark Osborn, a man who is always three weeks behind in all ideas even when he's at his brightest, began to poach on my preserves, as it were. Or emulate my methods. If one woos one should woo with the stamp of one's own personality, as I'm sure your Mr. Turnbull would agree."

"Never mind my Mr. Turnbull. How did it start?"

"I have a distinct impression that I would not like to be a policeman," said Talbot, and dabbed at his split lip. The cold water was almost blood red, now, and he still looked a mess. "You have to stick to the point so distressingly tightly, it must get you down at times. But I cannot tell a lie. For three months I have pledged myself to Regina, showering her with gifts which I cannot really afford. The oaf Osborn suddenly decided that he would send her chocolates."

Roger turned away abruptly.

"Lend me that towel, will you?" Talbot dabbed. "Thanks. I suppose, being dispassionate and all that, there was no cardinal crime in Mark sending her a box of chocs, and I can't honestly claim that the idea of sending chocolates and flowers to my love is a unique and original concept. But by a process of trial and error I did discover that the chocolates Regina prefers are Garry's. Not surprising, since Garry makes the best chocolates in the world. So when Mark is clod enough to send her Garry chocolates, the first time he's ever thought of doing it, well—my restraint broke."

"How do you know he did?"

"I saw the box on his desk last night. Garry's postal packing, Regina's address on the label."

"Why not punch Osborn on the nose last night?"

"He wasn't there. I left in a huff. I managed to keep my temper with praiseworthy self-control, too. We were polite to each other today. Tonight, he duly arrived here and I suppose I was bitter. Regina had said a firm 'no, she wouldn't dine,' and I haven't forgotten that she did dine with Mark. So I asked him why he hadn't brought me some chocolates. Just a little gentle nastiness. I thought it would soar way above his head, but he took it as neatly as he takes catches in the slips. He promptly answered back, and to cut a long story in half, he then attempted to bonk me one. I hit back. I don't mind telling you," went on Talbot, fingering his throat, "that I thought he was going to kill me two ways. I actually wondered how you would deal with that—I mean, which would you hang him for, strangling me or throwing me out of the window?"

He could be flippant; but he couldn't hide the fear of the death which had passed so closely by.

"How did you stop him?"

"To express myself graphically but coarsely, I kicked him in the guts. We then behaved like savages *avec* battle-axes. At least, I had a battle-ax. Er—West."

"Yes."

"I know, I'm prejudiced. I should think defending counsel could tear anything I said in court to bits, by bringing evidence of my desire to put Mark Osborn in the dirt. But seriously—he meant to kill me. Not when he arrived—at least I couldn't see the glitter in his eyes—but once we'd started, there was the old blood-lust."

144

"Possibly. These chocolates," Roger said. "How many boxes were there?"

"Damn it. One."

"Sure it was addressed to Miss Howard?"

"*Sans* a ha'porth of doubt."

"And you don't know of anyone else to whom he sends chocolates?"

"The grammar is impeccable, but the point of the question is a little misty," Talbot said. "He has ever been what I am now—a one-woman man. I—but wait."

He leaned forward and emptied the hand basin, then washed out the sponge and dabbed his lips again. He looked much more presentable, but his right eye was closing up, and both eyes were bloodshot.

"Still thinking up what to say next?"

"I like to get your facts right for you," Talbot declared. "Also, I think I have done Mark an injustice. Lor' love a duck, what would Mum think of her little Derek after this one? Oh lor', oh lor', oh lor'! As a matter of fact, I think it was Wilf's idea. Remember Wilf Dickerson? Each month we send a box of Garry's chocolates to each of the prize-winners, it was part of the prize, just a little added thought, you know, to keep all the little honeys sweet. I wouldn't mind betting that they were sent off yesterday, and Mark had the bright notion of taking Regina's along. Certainly they were on his desk. Check up, Mr. C.I.D. man." Talbot sat back on the stool and took out cigarettes. "Smoke? I need some soothing weed or drink, anyhow. I've got to think up some excuse for not apologizing to Mark. Got a light? Ta."

Mark Osborn was sitting in an armchair when Roger went into the other room. He hadn't suffered much damage, just a bruise on his right cheek. He looked composed enough, and told much the same story as Talbot, briefly, dully. He said yes, the monthly box of chocolates to each Queen had been sent off the previous day, and he'd kept Regina's back to hand to her in person, then found he couldn't see her that night and posted it at the last minute.

Sending the chocolates in the first place had been Dickerson's idea.

They were always Garry's chocolates.

Question and answer had reached that stage when Turnbull rang up, his voice humming with excitement.

"Hi, Handsome! That wrapping paper was smothered in Mark Osborn's fingerprints, and there were some of Talbot's, too. You haven't let 'em get away, I hope."

"Nothing's simply what it appears to be," Roger said dryly. "Anything else?"

"Isn't that enough?" Turnbull almost roared the question, then went on with a rush, "No, sergeant, it isn't! Alice Harvey's *dead* of poisoning. They got her to the hospital just too late. Barbara Kelworthy received some chocs, but didn't start them because she's had a bit of gastric flu. Norma Dearing never touches chocolates because of her figure, so she hasn't eaten her lot, either. At least no more harm will come from that damned attempt. I've been onto the hospital, by the way, your brats aren't doing so badly. Ptomaine, not arsenic! Also the Chelsea Division. They've found some kids—

one a son of a sergeant there, Morgan—who were playing with your pair this evening. Down by the river; you want to tan their hides. This Morgan lad found a packet of sandwiches and handed them round. That's the cause, all right."

"Yes, it's the answer," Roger agreed, "but your hunch came off." He didn't tell Turnbull what he knew about Osborn and Talbot, but went on, "We've got to get those chocolates analyzed, go through Conway's with a fine-toothed comb, and check everyone remotely connected with the job. What we haven't got to do is lose our heads."

Turnbull roared: "Are you telling me that I—"

He broke off, gulped, and broke off. There was a long silence, before Turnbull said, "Okay, so I lost my head over Regina. I can find it again, can't I? But listen. There are three Queens left out of seven. Just three left. Who's going next, and how's she going?"

16

Three Queens Left

The *Globe*, always the shrillest of the newspapers on this case, had huge headlines; a third of its front page said starkly:

FOURTH

QUEEN

DIES

and the rest was devoted to the story of the chocolates, Conway's monthly habit of sending them to the prize-winners, to everything connected with the case.

All the boxes sent out that week had been opened, every chocolate analyzed. Most had a tiny arsenic content introduced through a hole, pinhole size. One or two showed signs that an attempt had been made to dissolve the arsenic, but the poisoner had quickly discovered that the powder was insoluble. None of the chocolates had fingerprints.

The Yard added another quest to the search for

Dickerson; had he bought arsenic? They spread the inquiries to everyone connected with the case.

Roger spent an hour in the little workshop behind Garry's chocolate shop near Bond Street. The air was thick with the cloying fumes of chocolate and sugar, girls in spotless white smocks and caps worked busily or answered questions. All the chocolates were handmade. The boxes which had been sent to Conway's had been the usual kind, not made especially. They were always delivered to Conway's by hand, a two-pound box for each Queen.

No one at Garry's had seen a stranger at the shop or in the manufactory the day before.

The messenger boy who delivered said that he had put them on the desk at the inquiry office at Bennis Square, as usual. The girl in charge had been talking to someone on the telephone; that was all he remembered. Then came a moment almost of satisfaction for the Yard; there was a confusion of dates, the chocolates had in fact been left at Conway's inquiry office for the whole of one night, when anyone could have got at them.

The hunt for anyone who had been at the Conway building after the usual hours began.

Dickerson could have been there. So could Talbot, so could Osborn; but there was no proof that any one of these had. Arsenic wasn't traced to anyone, either.

The lines of inquiry were gradually closed up, the only one still open was the hunt for Dickerson. Every newspaper ran his photograph again. He looked such a mild, diffident, kindly little man.

Wilfrid Dickerson the Trustworthy, Wilfrid Dickerson the old family friend of the Howards, the

Impersonal, became the embodiment of evil to millions. The innocent-looking face seemed to alter when one stared at it, the wrinkled forehead sprouted horns, the tone of the newspapers, defying the risk of later contempt of court, condemned him without trial.

The newspapers changed from full support of the police to sharp criticism; the *Globe*'s reward was increased from £500 to £1,500. Still there was no trace of Dickerson, or of any one of the people involved, buying arsenic or anything which had an arsenic content.

Every man's body discovered anywhere in the British Isles, and which might conceivably be that of the missing Beauty Competition expert, was measured and checked, but Dickerson wasn't found either dead or alive.

Conway's postponed the next competition; at least there was breathing space, and the Yard had to accept the blow to its prestige.

Of the three Queens who were left alive, only Regina lived a normal life. She saw Turnbull most days; and she seemed to steer an even course between him and the other two suitors.

Norma Dearing, who lived in a Kentish suburb, gave up her work as a photographer's model, hugged her home, and never went out alone. The *Globe* and other papers ran heart-rending stories of the effect on her nerves. Barbara Kelworthy, of Wembley, did much the same. The Divisional police watched them both, the Yard watched them, the public and the Press watched them. They became almost like royalty in their own right, could hardly move without the spotlight of publicity.

Neither was attacked.

The police watched Regina's home, and one Yard man always followed her, but she seemed almost oblivious. Her beauty had a serenity which nothing really disturbed. Somehow she managed to resist the sensationalism that the Press tried to create for her. After a few days they gave up trying much with her, and concentrated on the other two.

But West, who also saw Regina most days, was quite sure that the fears were buried deep in her eyes. How could she fail to feel fear, unless—

There was one obvious explanation: if she felt none; if her naturalness came because she no longer believed that she had cause for fear. That explanation was so simple that it would have been easy to overlook it. Regina would not be afraid if she *knew* that she was no longer in danger.

If she knew that, then she also knew from whom the danger threatened.

The attack on her might even have been faked—

Conway's, being a powerful combine, with many subsidiaries, had much influence. Some of this they exerted, soon after the *Globe*'s latest sensational stories, and from a highly important member of the Government it reached Chatworth; and from him, Roger.

"Conway's are belly-aching," Chatworth said briefly and bluffly. "This scandal is costing them a fortune. All show cards, press publicity, wrappers, and cartons have to be scrapped because the faces on them are those dead girls. Business, of course, is business. They're sorry about the girls, but wish they hadn't started the Competition because of the money it's costing." Chatworth looked down his nose. "Mind you, I can see their point of view.

151

They're not selling as much soap as they like. It's having a boomerang effect."

Roger didn't speak.

"Between you and me, they're behind the rewards being offered," Chatworth went on. "They're trying to stir up the Home Office, and force us to get results. You'd better let me have a good, smooth report to show how we're running the job."

"If there's an angle I like," growled Roger, "it's being prodded that way."

But he could understand it.

Regina walked briskly up the stairs leading to her office ten days after the death of the fourth Queen. By coincidence, it was also the day when the West children were to be released from hospital. She went into her office. The proprietor was in France, and as always she had a lot to do. But she was thinking more about Derek and Mark, who would undoubtedly come in before long.

It was nearly ten o'clock.

The morning mail hadn't been opened. Regina slit the envelopes one by one, then began to take out the letters. Most were addressed to the little company, a few to her personally. She knew about fan letters to the Queens, who had become used to absurdities: to offers of marriage out of the blue, offers of a stage career, weird and wonderful propositions, requests for autographs and photographs, letters from schoolboys and schoolgirls, from Lonely Hearts and Solitary Sailors; from the forgotten, the lonely, the sad, the eccentric, and the mad. She had already had her share.

She took one out of an envelope addressed to herself. As she unfolded it, there was a sharp crack like the crack of a Christmas cracker, a flash, and a puff of smoke.

"Oh!" she screamed, and jumped up, her heart hammering, her throat suddenly tight.

The letter lay on the desk, the wisp of smoke fading and the sparks already gone. A girl came running in from another office, and started as Regina gazed in terror at the paper. This had a small burn mark in it, like a cigarette burn or an indoor firework.

That's all it was, she tried to tell herself; a silly practical joke.

There were thudding footsteps, and Mark Osborn rushed in.

"Gina!" he cried. "Gina, what is it?" He leaped to her. Her pallor would have startled anyone, and it seemed to horrify him. "Oh, God, Gina!" He held her in his arms, crushing her to him. "I can't let this keep on happening," he said hoarsely, "I just can't let it go on. These damned inefficient policemen, the doddering fools, what do they think they are? Why don't they get the swine? Why don't they get him?"

He was shouting hoarsely.

"Mark, don't—"

"If they can't, I will," cried Osborn. "I'll find out who the murdering devil is, and I'll kill him with my own hands. I'll save you, Gina, I'll make sure no one can attack you again." He was still holding her tightly, as if he would not let her go.

"I know you will, Mark," she said, very gently.

Then Talbot came in.

He stood looking on, the color fading from his cheeks, a strange expression creeping into his eyes. Then the girl who had rushed in when she had heard Regina cry out told him what had happened. The look in Talbot's eyes changed. He

153

moved toward Mark and Regina, and said lightly, "Break, folk, the party's over."

He picked up the letter, and for the first time the others noticed him. He looked at them both, then back at the letter, and read in a strained voice:

"You'll go when your time comes, Queenie."

"Friendly little missive," he said, in a lighter voice. "Has anyone sent for that chap West?"

"There's no clue on the envelope except the postmark London W.C.," Roger said to Turnbull. "The paper's ordinary cream-laid, you can buy it almost anywhere. The only fingerprints were the postman's and the office boy's who took the mail into Regina's office. In other words, another blank."

"It could have blinded her," Turnbull growled.

"Not likely," Roger said. "Most people hold an envelope eighteen inches or so away from the face when opening it. The amount of explosive was negligible, too. This was a scare letter."

"If I could get my hands round—" Turnbull began, but didn't finish, just raised his big, well-shaped, and powerful hands. Then he relaxed. "Okay, okay, I'm losing control! As Osborn. He's showing up a bit screwy, isn't he?"

"Living on his nerves, yes. We've always known the killer could kill again if he wanted to," Roger said evenly. "But everything he does helps us a bit. He was able to get some white arsenic. He could manufacture that exploding letter—"

"Pooh, easy," Turnbull said; "anyone with a few fireworks and a bit of spirit gum could fix a thing like that."

"He's clever with his hands. The way he inserted the arsenic shows that, too. A man with a lot of patience, who knows exactly what he wants, and—"

"Okay—Dickerson."

Roger said, "I've a nasty feeling we might come across Dickerson's body. Don't forget the way this started. We were nearly fooled by Millsom. The man who was up in that steeple with Millsom shot at me, remember, and then pushed Millsom over and thought he'd fooled us."

"He fooled *me*." Turnbull was almost vicious as he said that. "Handsome, every time I think of Harold Millsom I want to know why he ran away, if he didn't kill Betty Gelibrand."

"So do I."

"Had another go at his pa?"

Roger said, surprised, "The vicar of St. Cleo's?"

"Yep. Just because a man has a dog collar he isn't a saint or proof against crime," Turnbull said. "I think he could tell us why young Millsom ran to him—if he would."

"I'll drop in soon, and try again," Roger said. "Let's get back to this: we were nearly fooled at St. Cleo's. The man who fooled us may be repeating the tactics. Dickerson fits into our puzzle, so kill Dickerson, hide the body, and then sit back and laugh while we waste our time trying to find him," Roger went on. "I get tired of coming back to the same place, but we have to. If the motive we're toying with is the right one, then someone closely associated with one of the Queens is behind it, and we can't find anyone who is backing Barbara Kelworthy or Norma Dearing."

"Right back where we started from," Turnbull

crooned. "Talbot and Osborn. Every spare minute I've got, I watch 'em. And we always have them tailed. But since that last fight of theirs, they haven't put a foot wrong. Did you know that Regina's patched up things between them?"

"Yes."

Turnbull said, as if sneeringly, "Nice girl, Regina. Sweet disposition. I don't mind admitting that I fell for the beauty. But I'm beginning to wonder. She's almost too good to be true. One strangler who might have meant to fool us. One explosive envelope and a threat, causing no harm. And she's cool as ice."

Roger kept a straight face.

"Think so?"

"I'm asking you."

"If you mean, do I think that Regina's behind it herself, and that explains how calm she keeps, I don't think I do." Roger wasn't surprised by Turnbull's look of relief. "She's no fool, and if she were in it I think she'd play being scared. Actually I think she really is scared, but won't give way to it."

"For mama's sake?"

"That's it."

"If there's a situation I think is criminal, it's when a girl throws herself away on an old and sick woman. It ought to be punishable by law."

"Well, it isn't," Roger said. "Don't you try punishing it yourself. She's a pleasant enough old soul, and I don't know that Regina Howard wants to get married and settle down. She may be a career woman!" The telephone bell rang, and he lifted it. "Hallo?"

156

"Detective Constable Marriott would like a word with you, sir," the girl operator said.

"Put him through. Marriott?" repeated Roger. "Marriott? Do I know—"

"Jake Marriott? The man who's trailing Regina." Turnbull looked at it as if he would like to snatch the telephone away.

Roger said into the mouthpiece, "Yes, Marriott?"

"I thought I'd better call you yourself, sir," Marriott said, and his voice betrayed his anxiety. "I've lost Miss Howard. A car cut in on me and then I had to stop at some lights. I was stuck. Couldn't pick her up again."

"Where was this?"

"Corner of Edgware Road and Pillen Street—not so very far from where she lives. She'd gone home in the middle of the morning, first time I've known her to do that. I parked at the end of the street, and followed as usual."

"All right, Marriott," Roger said. "Come back here, will you?" He rang off, irritated by Turnbull's demanding gaze. He told Turnbull, while lifting the telephone again. "Information Room—I want a search made for Regina Howard, you have her description, last seen at the corner of Edgware Road and Pillen Street driving her own Austin Seven, dark blue, 1946 model, registration number—"

"We've got that, sir."

"Thanks. Make it snappy."

"We will, sir."

Roger rang off. Turnbull wiped his forehead.

That was at half-past twelve; ten minutes later, Osborn's tailer reported that Osborn had given him the slip. A call went out for Osborn in a hurry.

By half-past five a dozen people had rung up to

say that Regina was missing. At twenty to six, word came that Talbot was waiting in the hall, demanding to see Roger personally.

There was no sign of Regina or of her car.

The *Evening Globe* splashed it in huge letters:

ANOTHER QUEEN MISSING

Roger called the Hall Sergeant.

"Send Mr. Talbot up," he said, "and see that he has company all the way."

"Yes, sir."

Eddie Day looked round, but didn't speak, and no one else was in the office. Turnbull had been out for the past two hours. Roger lit a cigarette and looked unseeingly at the plane trees and the sunshine and the little corner of the roof of the London County Hall building visible from here. Then the door opened, and Talbot came in; a pale-brown tailor's model.

He was trying to smile.

"*Sanctum sanctorum,*" he said. "I won't violate unduly. Thing is, I have information of importance which you probably won't believe."

Eddie Day gave up pretending to work, and stared.

"Try me," Roger said.

"Osborn lured her away," Talbot said. "I have what I regard as proof. I know I'm prejudiced, but look at the way my pal Mark is behaving. Apart from nearly strangling me, he is the nu in neurosis. I'm told that he almost suffocated Regina when he rushed in to the rescue this morning. Would you, as a great detective, have heard of the unfortunate mental affliction known as schizophrenia?'"

158

"Where's this evidence you're talking about?"

"I also can detect. We've some direct-line call boxes, and Mark Osborn was heard to telephone Gina after she'd gone home this morning. Her mother had a nasty heart attack, but pulled through all right. Intelligent and persistent questioning of the staff uncovered news of this telephone conversation. Mark said something about having to see Gina for lunch, life and death, all that balderdash. She fell. She was always rather soft-spotted for him. No, I don't know where they went. But I'm terrified of what might happen to her while with him."

His eyes told the truth of that; terror was in him.

17

Action

There were days, there were weeks, when nothing would go right; then suddenly everything would fall into place and hopes would surge. The first crack in the case came while Derek Talbot stood staring at Roger, convincing him that he was terrified for Regina—and of Mark Osborn.

The telephone bell rang.

Roger lifted the receiver. "Hallo?"

"We've traced that Austin Seven," Turnbull announced like a squall of wind. "Garden of an empty house, Paddington, believe it or not. Can you come?"

"You go ahead. Keep in touch by radio." Roger put down the receiver sharply. "I've a job to do," he said to Talbot.

"Can I come along?"

Roger said, "No. Officially, no."

He gave a fleeting grin, and moved toward the door, grabbing his hat as he passed the stand. Excitement helped to drive fear out of Talbot's eyes. He followed, and when Roger and Sergeant Dalby were moving in Roger's car, Talbot in a taxi was on their heels.

Roger headed for Paddington, a narrow street and an exclusive little restaurant. It was closed. He stood rat-tatting at the door when Talbot pulled up in his taxi. Talbot didn't get out. A sallow-faced man in a white apron came to the door at last. There was a smell of garlic hovering about him.

"Yes, what ees it?"

"Mr. Popacuros, please," Roger said, and showed a card which silenced the man's protests.

Roger and Dalby went in; Talbot, uninvited but not barred, followed. The rooms looked tiny, the tables bare, stacked chairs stood on several of them, the cutlery was missing.

Mr. Popacuros, the patron, appeared at the foot of a flight of narrow stairs, struggling to get into a pale-blue coat. He was plump, earnest, and sleepy —his eyes looked as if they wouldn't keep open.

"But, Chief Inspector, nothing has happened here, I—"

"Was Mr. Mark Osborn in to lunch?"

"Mr. Osborn? But yes!"

"By himself?"

"No, indeed, he was not by himself," said Popacuros, "he was with ze lady—" He paused and flickered a glance of recognition at Talbot, and looked very unhappy. "He was with ze lady who was with him ze other evening, when—"

"What time did they leave?"

"About three o'clock, Chief Inspector."

"By car?"

"Yes, but not his usual one. It was a new kind,

what is the word, yes, a Bristol!" Mr. Popacuros looked delighted with himself.

"What color?" asked Roger.

"Gray, I am sure."

"Thanks very much," said Roger. "I want to know what you or any of the staff heard them say —have a chat with Sergeant Dalby here, will you?" He was casual, hoping that his manner would woo Popacuros into making a statement, even a casual word overheard might be valuable.

He smiled thanks and turned past Talbot, who hurried after him. He slid into his car and flicked on the radio.

The Yard answered.

"Put out a general call for a gray Bristol car, find out how Mark Osborn got it, if you can. It was last seen . . ." He went on, briskly.

Talbot was listening, just behind him.

"Good," Roger said. "What's the address of the place where Detective Inspector Turnbull went? . . . Thanks. Send him a flash that I'm on my way." He switched the walkie-talkie off, and looked at Talbot. "I suppose there's no law against giving you a lift."

"You might think of one just when I need it most," Talbot said. "I'll keep to my cab, *merci*. Don't go too fast."

He scurried off.

The Austin had been found in a yard at the back of a house which had once been used as builders' and decorators' premises. Bomb damage had been too great for repair. One blackened wall was shored up by huge beams. A rubble of bricks and slate and broken concrete filled the garden, bravely covered by wild flowers and spindly grass.

The Austin Seven had been driven over some of this and stood close to the house, leaning precariously to one side. Turnbull was bending inside it, and looked all massive posterior.

Talbot came nimbly over the rubble.

"This is the one moment of my life when I'd give a fortune for a camera."

"I didn't know you had a fortune."

"What a horror you must be to live with." Talbot stared at Turnbull, who drew back from the car looking very red in the face; but he hadn't lost any confidence.

He gave Roger a mock salute, and sent a hard, unfriendly glare at Talbot.

"Last driven by Osborn," he announced; "I've checked fingerprints. Th girl's are there too, but a lot of her prints are obliterated. So, hunt for Osborn."

"That's what we're doing," Roger said. "Anything else inside that Austin?"

"I don't think so."

"Gentlemen," Talbot said, in a thin voice. "Or policemen. Mark sent the deadly chocs. Mark is a bad case of neurosis. Mark loves Regina more than life itself, he says, but—"

"Shut up," Turnbull growled.

"No. For the love of Mike, find them. If you'd seen the way he changed, seen the look in his eyes when he started to strangle me the other night, you'd know what I mean. I don't say he's insane, but—"

"I said shut up!"

Roger pretended to be interested only in the Austin Seven, and not to notice. Turnbull was a

163

Goliath against Talbot, who was absurdly slender, but who faced the Yard man without flinching.

"If the day ever comes when I take any notice of you," he said, "I shall apply for a death certificate."

They glared at each other....

If the truth was what it appeared to be, in their different ways they were distraught because of Regina Howard.

Roger moved away, and reached his own car. Two Yard men were searching the builders' yard, but none of these spoke. Roger flicked on the radio again, and the Yard answered.

"Anything on Osborn's Bristol?"

"He hired it from his usual garage, his M.G. had valve trouble. Flash just come in, sir, hold on...." There was a pause long enough for Talbot to come toward Roger and Turnbull to light a cigarette. "Hallo, sir....The car's been seen on the Hog's Back, near Guildford—that was at four twenty-five, sir. A man driving, girl passenger. The Surrey police are checking, so are the Hampshire chaps. That's all, sir."

"Good, thanks." Another day, it might have been hours before they'd had a word, this was beginning to look good.

Talbot burst out, "Any luck?"

"Yes. You'd better come with me." Turnbull heard that, and fumed in silent protest. "You follow, will you? We're heading for Guildford; might pick up something else there or on the way."

"Right." Turnbull was on the move at once.

"Get in the back, Talbot, will you?" Roger got into his car. Dalby sat next to him. Talbot almost fell in and slammed the door.

"Damned good of you, West."

164

"Just as well to keep you under my eye," Roger said gruffly. He threaded his way across London to Hammersmith, and then had a clear run to Putney, the Heath, Roehampton, and the sweeping Kingston by-pass. There was little traffic on the six-lane highway stretches. Halfway along, Dalby picked up the radio phone, at a sign from Roger.

"Speaking for Inspector West—"

A disembodied voice came into the car.

"Message waiting, sir, please hold on....Hallo, Chief Inspector West....Gray Bristol car registration ALK 5143 found in a copse near Higley, Surrey—off the Hog's Back...Guildford patrol car waiting there to guide you."

"All clear," Dalby said, and for once he couldn't keep excitement out of his voice. "They've found him, sir!"

From the back, Talbot, "West, I know the one about little boys. But if I'm right, Mark's deadly. He could scar Regina's mind for life, even if he didn't do a thing to her, and he might kill—"

He broke off.

Roger said, "We'll handle this as if we know he'll try to kill. Just sit back, will you?"

Talbot might be right, and Osborn might be the killer. If he was, if it was a case of a split mind, then there was no way of guessing what might happen now. If the man were Osborn and he had fired at Roger from the roof of St. Cleo's he would probably be armed, and he would probably shoot again.

Talbot couldn't relax, just sat on the edge of his seat.

Turnbull kept on Roger's tail, pressing too close.

They reached Higley at half-past six, had a brief word with the patrol-car men, and followed to the cottage and the copse where Mark Osborn had arrived with Regina nearly an hour and a half earlier.

That much was known for certain. No one could be quite sure that the couple hadn't left again, but the Bristol was still in the copse, hidden by trees and bushes. So the couple was probably inside the cottage.

The police hadn't shown themselves yet.

"I'm going straight to the front door," Roger said to Turnbull and the little group of Surrey policemen. "You make a ring round the place. Talbot, you stay back here, out of sight. If anyone's likely to sent Osborn off his head, you are." He ignored Turnbull's mumbled agreement. "All clear?"

"Why should you go?" Turnbull demanded. "Why not let me—"

"My job," Roger said briefly. "You take the back door."

The men moved round, taking cover near bushes and behind a beech hedge. The sun burned down, and there was no cloud anywhere. The cottage lay in a dell, with a small oval lawn and an old-world garden in front of it, a blaze of color. The paths were of grass, a little overgrown. No other building was in sight, except a few tiny outhouses. There were the country sounds and the quiet and a kind of lurking menace.

Then Roger saw Osborn's face appear at the window, and knew that Osborn realized that someone was there.

Osborn stood by the window, with a gun in his right hand, his eyes narrowed, his lips parted so that he looked as if he were snarling. Regina, tied by the waist to a chair, was in a corner away from the window, where it was very gloomy. Creeper round the window kept much of the sunlight out, but there was sweat on Osborn's forehead, and Regina felt insufferably hot.

"Mark, don't do anything," she pleaded; "whoever it is, don't use that gun."

"I told you what I'd do," Osborn said. "I'll kill anyone who tries to take you away from me. Understand, I'll *kill* him. Now I've got you, at last I've got you." He gave a sudden, shrill, frightening laugh. "It's what I ought to have done months ago —just picked you up and carried you away! That's how they used to behave in the old days, isn't it?" He tore his glance away from the window and stared at her. "If you knew what you do to me, if you knew how your beauty *hurts* me—"

"Mark, put that gun away. Don't do anything silly."

"Silly?" He gave a different laugh, just a harsh bark. "Never been so sane in my life. Sane and sensible. I've got you away from them all—from the killer *and* from Derek. Do you know what I think? I think they're one and the same. You didn't think of that, did you? *Derek's* the devil. I'm not surprised, I—"

"Mark, be reasonable," Regina pleaded. The sweat made her forehead, her cheeks, and her nose shiny, and every now and again she bit her lips, but she managed to keep her voice very steady. "Derek's too fond of me—"

"He's followed you, that's all!"

"Well—well, perhaps you're right," Regina said, as if he had persuaded her. "But if you are, then we ought to tell the police. That's the sensible thing to do."

"Think you can fool me, don't you?" He stared out of the window, at the still branches of the trees and the glorious colors of the flowers and the off-green of the lawns, which badly needed water. "I've finished with the police, understand. I'm going to look after you myself, *I'm* the only one I can trust. I'll show everyone I mean business."

He laughed again.

Regina shivered, and felt hotter; choking.

"Everyone knows how smart you are, Mark, but don't make trouble for yourself. If you shoot—"

He turned to face her. There was a strange light in his eyes, a light which seemed to burn. He shook his head very slowly. For a moment, he seemed to forget that there were men outside, watching, waiting their chance to come.

"Even you don't know what's good for you," he said. "Sometimes I think you've been deceiving me. Well, get this clear, Gina. I've got you. No one's going to take you away from me. The killer, the police, that suave hypocrite Talbot, let 'em all come. Rather than let them have you, I'd kill you. Understand? I'd kill us both."

She didn't answer.

Then a sound broke the silent stillness, and he turned and saw Roger West coming through the garden gate.

18

Intent to Kill

The gate closed behind Roger.

Regina could not see outside, but she could see the way in which Osborn moved the gun upward, pointing it at someone out of the window. She could see his lips turned back, showing his teeth. She knew, now, that he wasn't really himself, that nothing she could say would influence him. She'd made a dreadful mistake in coming with him, hoping to humor and to help him. Now he had the gun in his hand, and his mind was filled with intent to kill.

The window was open at the top.

If she screamed, she would warn and save the man outside, wouldn't she? The footsteps drew nearer. Whoever it was came quite briskly, as if he had not the slightest idea that danger waited for him. He couldn't be far away, now, and Mark was a good shot, Mark wouldn't miss. He stood on one side so that he could see out but could not be seen, with the gun waist high.

The footsteps drew nearer. The gun moved slowly, menacingly.

"*Be careful!*" she screamed, "*he's armed, he's armed!*"

She saw Osborn flinch at the first cry, next heard a scrabble of footsteps, then suddenly the bark of the gun. There were two flashes of flame as glass crashed. The footsteps still sounded, but there had been no cry.

"He got away," Osborn said hoarsely. "He got away." He turned and looked at her. His eyes were dazed, and for the first time she dared to hope. "Missed him," he said stupidly. "But I—"

He caught his breath, and the dullness faded from his eyes, they became bright and angry.

"You warned him," he said roughly. "You shouldn't have done that Gina. I told you that if I couldn't have you, no one else could."

He seemed to be suspended in some half-world which he did not properly understand himself. He glanced out of the window, back to her, out of the window again; and then he stiffened.

"There's Talbot!" he barked. "I told you so, it's Talbot! He's the devil. He's got others with him. They won't get you, I won't let them get you, no one shall have—"

The door crashed back.

Regina saw the massive bulk of Turnbull hurtle forward. Osborn had his back to the window and the gun in his hand and the intent to kill in his eyes. Death would never be nearer the Yard man until it caught up with him. He didn't utter a sound.

It was over so quickly, but seemed to last so long.

First, Osborn with the gun still rising; then Turnbull moving; then the roar of the gun and the flash; then the two men colliding, and Osborn carried back against the window with a crash which deafened her. But through the roaring in her ears there were other sounds; voices, thumping footsteps, banging doors. Regina saw Osborn and Turnbull on the floor, Turnbull on top, Turnbull smashing at Osborn's face with his clenched fist. The gun was lying by the wall, out of reach. Turnbull was just hitting at Osborn, whose face was suddenly blotched with red and then smeared and then a red mess....

Men rushed in.

Roger West was among them, and it was West who bent down, grabbed the gun, and cracked the butt on Osborn's head. Osborn collapsed and lay on the floor, moaning, twisting his body about, bleeding at the lips, the temple, and the cheeks. Turnbull's clothes, as well as Osborn's, were spattered with blood. He got up unsteadily.

Talbot appeared.

"Gina," he said in a choky voice. "Gina." He was with her in a flash, in front of her, taking her hands. Then he dropped to his knees, and almost sobbed. "You're all right, thank God, you're all right." The grip of his hands hurt, but she didn't try to free herself. "I was so afraid," he said, "I was so afraid."

Then West, getting up from Osborn's side, discovered that Regina was tied to the chair.

With a doctor by his side, Osborn was on the way to London, in an ambulance. He had been given a shot of morphia, and was likely to be out for sev-

171

eral hours. Regina sat in the chair to which she had been fastened, tea in her hands. Talbot, strangely tongue-tied, was standing and looking at her, and the only word to describe the expression in his eyes was adoration.

Turnbull was at Guildford Hospital, with a flesh wound in his side. He had been able to walk to the car which had taken him, but had hardly said a word since the fight. Outside, police were searching for the spent bullets.

Now Roger was also drinking tea, a Guildford Inspector was with them, and the patient Dalby, phlegmatic again, had a notebook in his hand. Regina hadn't much color, and there was a shadow in her eyes. It seemed to hurt Talbot even to look at her.

"I suppose it was my own fault," she said. "Mark rang up when I was at home and said he simply had to see me, he had important news. So I met him for lunch, and he kept saying he was sure that —that you were the killer, Derek."

Talbot said weakly, "Not true."

"Of course it isn't true, but he believed it."

"Did he say what made him think so?" Roger asked.

"It was chiefly because of those chocolates," Regina said. "He'd seen Derek with them in his hand, the night before they were posted. He thought that Derek had switched them."

Talbot didn't speak.

"I could see he wasn't well, and tried to reason with him," Regina went on. "He kept saying that he just couldn't live without—"

"You," interpolated Talbot.

"Oh, it was absurd, but he seemed so desperately

in earnest, I had to try to help him. He suggested a spin in the country, and promised to telephone the office and say I'd be back late. We parked my car in a disused yard, then came down here. He said this cottage belonged to an old friend of his, and we could have some tea. Even then I didn't realize how far he'd lost his control," Regina went on very tensely. "I knew he wasn't normal and wasn't well, his eyes looked strange; burning. He said he had a bad headache. He insisted on putting the kettle on and told me to sit down—this chair was facing the window then." She closed her eyes, as if to shut out the memory. "The next thing I knew, he'd dropped a rope over me and was tying me up. He said it was the only way he could make sure that I never got away from him. He didn't really know what he was doing."

"Charity, charity," said Talbot huskily, "thine other name is Regina."

"He couldn't have known," she insisted. "It must have been a brainstorm."

She paused, and Dalby caught up with his short-hand notes and Roger poured out more tea.

"What else did he say?"

"It wasn't very sensible," Regina told him. "He wasn't going to let me go, he'd find the killer and kill him. That—that was always in his mind, finding the killer. Mr. West, I just don't believe that he's the man you want. I can't believe it."

"Oh, charity," murmured Talbot again.

The Yard seemed almost deserted at half-past nine that night. Roger sat alone at the desk, glad that no one else was there to harass him, checking the reports. Osborn had come round, and according to the interim report, was outwardly normal and did not remember what had happened—except that he had had a fight with Derek Talbot.

Roger had checked Osborn's own doctor and a police surgeon. Osborn had been sleeping badly, had obviously been living on his nerves for some time. A nervous collapse turned into a brainstorm was the likely medical verdict. Not common, but not exactly rare.

Turnbull would be off duty for three or four days at least; but his wound wasn't serious.

Regina was back with her mother, who did not know what had happened that afternoon, and was not to be told. The newspapers hadn't got the story, and no statement was made. There was still no news of Wilfrid Dickerson, although a dozen reports had come in only that day, reporting that he had been seen in a dozen different places.

The most significant items were about Osborn. Every possible double check was made on his movements, and now a summary was in front of Roger.

No one knew for certain where Osborn had been on the night of Betty Gelibrand's murder, but his movements on the night of Hilda Shaw's murder and on the afternoon of the chase at St. Cleo's proved that he could not have been at either place. It wouldn't matter if the Press and the public, including Derek Talbot, believed that he was the killer. There was no evidence at all. The bullets were a different size from the one fired at St. Cleo's.

Somewhere, hidden, unknown, the killer still lurked.

The one certain thing was that he mustn't be allowed to strike again.

A strong guard was placed at Regina Howard's home, at Barbara Kelworthy's, and at Norma Dearing's.

"Mum, it's no use," Barbara Kelworthy said. "I can't stand this any longer, I've just got to go out!"

She jumped up from a sofa in the small living room at her home near Wembley. There was a glowing, gypsy loveliness about her, brown, shining eyes, dark hair, a bright color which owed little to make-up. The same gypsy grace was in her movements, too, and a vitality which had helped her to win the once-coveted prize. She moved like quicksilver, and had a figure in ten thousand.

"I just *can't*, I say. I'm going to the pictures tonight. Gregory Peck's on, and I just won't miss it. So there," breathed Barbara.

"Well, dear," said her mother, "I expect one of those policemen would be glad to go along with you. I wouldn't mind going to the pictures myself for once." She was a faded woman with a spiritless smile. Her husband was in the merchant navy, and she was always vaguely surprised when he came home. Of all the parents who had been affected by the Beauty Queen murders, she had been the most placid. "Why don't you put on your new dress, dear, and—"

"But I don't want to go with a copper!"

"I'm sure they're quite nice men," her mother said. "They always thank me very nicely when I take them a cup of tea. In a way it's quite expensive, but—"

"Let 'em bring their own damned tea," Barbara

stormed. "Mum, be a sport, go and ask Charlie Wray if he'll take me out tonight. The very idea of holding hands with a copper makes me shiver! Now if it was that big shot, West, or the other inspector it wouldn't be so bad, but these flatfoots." She sniffed. "Go on, Mum, slip out and ask Charlie. If it's a question of money, I'll pay."

"When your father wanted to take me out, he always paid," said Mrs. Kelworthy reminiscently, "but all right, dear, you'll only get melancholy if you stay in all the time. Your Uncle Benny went melancholy, ever so funny it made him. But you'll have to let the policemen follow you, won't you?"

"Oh, it'd be easy, but I won't give them the slip," Barbara sneered.

Her mother went out....

Charlie Wray was not only eager to take the beautiful Barbara out, but he was in funds. Nothing but the best seats were good enough for Barbara. The police were promptly told. Two went ahead and two walked behind Barbara and her Charlie, who acquired a remarkable self-importance. He was a burly young man, personable enough, with a square chin and eyes which were ready to look the world in the face. As the procession went on, he felt as if he were doing exactly that. From the front doors of the houses in the street, from houses in streets round and about, from ground-floor, first-floor, and top-floor windows, people stared at Barbara. They stared with almost as much curiosity at the young man escorting her out on her first venture since the *Globe* had paid £250 for her "Story of My Terror."

Perhaps because the ponderous progress of the police put her off, perhaps because the crowd near the picture palace in the High Street was becoming a mob, Mrs. Kelworthy did not go to the pictures. So, the police did not follow her. They had a man at the front door of the house and another at the back, and they knew that Mrs. Kelworthy was having one or two at the Red Lion, a pub on a friendly corner.

When she came out again, as dusk gathered, she was with a slim, middle-aged woman in a neat gray suit, stout shoes, and, unexpectedly, a veil with a lot of little black blobs on it. No one was surprised or troubled. The constable at the front door did his duty, by greeting Mrs. Kelworthy with an amiable smile, and, "This lady a friend of yours, ma'am?"

"Friend of mine," echoed Mrs. Kelworthy, roundly. "I should think she is. And what's more, she's a friend of my husband's, too."

The constable grinned, knowing Sailor Kelworthy. The woman smiled behind her black-bobbed veil. The door of the little house closed upon the pair. Mrs. Kelworthy promptly put on a kettle and then showed "her husband's friend" over the house; she was a little confused, and probably could not have told anyone on oath whether she had met the other woman previously.

It had not in fact been a chance acquaintance at the Red Lion that night. . . .

Mrs. Kelworthy was very proud of her Barbara. The small parlor and the girl's bedroom were smothered with her photographs and photographs of gatherings where she had competed.

The "friend" was greatly impressed.

Then a bubbling sound attracted their attention, and Mrs. Kelworthy rushed down the narrow stairs, to discover that the kettle was boiling. Her loud laughter sounded through the house, and she took the trouble to come to the foot of the stairs and shout up, "It's all right, dear, only the kettle. You 'ave a good look!"

"I won't be long," called the "friend." "Down in two ticks."

The constable outside the front door heard all this. Nothing could have sounded more innocuous. He heard footsteps, too, and now and again Mrs. Kelworthy's laughter. He wasn't surprised that she had had one or two more than she could stand, at the Lion. She had been under a great strain, and had taken it remarkably well.

The night was quiet.

The quiet was broken, a little before eleven, by an unfamiliar rumbling and muttering and clattering. At least two hundred people followed Barbara and Charlie home. They jammed the narrow street—in fact, there was hardly room for the little, veiled middle-aged woman to squeeze through and get away, although she managed to with remarkable agility and some vigor.

The police closed the door.

The general feeling was that now that the ice was broken, Barbara would be able to breathe more freely. Not a man among the police on guard dreamed that there was any danger to her that night; most would have said, quite confidently, that nothing would ever happen to her while they were at hand.

Mrs. Kelworthy went to sleep.

Barbara, with dreams of film stardom freshened, also went to sleep, happier than she had been for a long time. Charlie was quite nice, really.

She did not notice the smoke.

The room was at the top of the house, and the window overlooked the roofs of houses at the back. It was so placed that the constable on duty in an alleyway behind the house could not see it very well, and certainly he did not see the smoke which began to creep out of it, a little after three o'clock.

The flames weren't seen for another two hours, by which time it was daylight.

19

Death by Suffocation

There was a constable at the back, getting tired and feeling chilly, and wondering whether he should smoke another cigarette in the quiet of his corner or whether he would walk to the end of the alleyway and back.

A red glow showed against the window of a house adjacent to the Kelworthys'. The constable stared at it, thinking that it looked as if someone had an electric fire on in the room—a bathroom wall fire, for instance. Then he noticed that the glow wasn't steady.

He caught his breath.

After a moment he raced to the end of the alley and crashed open the gate of the little back garden. From there the smoke showed thick and gray against the morning sky, and he could see the flames.

His whistle shrilled.

The back door was locked and bolted. He didn't waste time over that, but jumped onto the sill of the ground-floor window, then pulled himself up to

Barbara's room, hanging on by his fingers and clawing at the wall with his feet. Now he saw flames burning fiercely in a corner, and could feel the heat. Smoke rolled out and threatened to suffocate him, but he managed to get a foot against a drainpipe, and keep himself steady while pushing up the window.

By then, other police had arrived.

The constable opened the window wide enough to get inside the room. He almost fell. The flames were making an inferno of a corner beneath the bed. He could see the girl amid the swirling smoke —lying quite still on her side; she looked so beautiful.

He lifted her off the bed.

Other police had run a ladder up to the window.

Gasping for breath, eyes watering, hair singed and uniform scorched, the policeman got Barbara to the window, and then other police took over. The girl didn't move. Neighbors were already at their windows, and a *Globe* reporter, who had a bed-sitting room in the front of a house opposite, came staggering out, bleary-eyed, unable to believe that he had been sleeping at the vital moment.

They carried Barbara into the house next door and applied artificial respiration, while the police started to put the fire out, and the fire brigade finished the job. A scared, tearful, bleary-eyed Mrs. Kelworthy kept asking where her Barbara was, and then crying, "There's a fire, I can smell it, something's burning!"

It wasn't until doctors had tried desperately to save Barbara's life and given up all hope, that her mother was told the truth. Barbara was as dead as the other four Queens, and had died by suffocation.

"That's the end," Turnbull growled thickly. "That's the beginning and the end." They were back at the Yard after a hurried visit to the Kelworthy house. "They let the killer go in and start a fire, and then make a path for her to get out through the crowd. That's the biggest laugh I've heard. That ought to earn the damned coppers a George Medal."

He was almost purple with rage.

"It's one of the few ways it could have happened," Roger said gruffly. "We can't close everything up, there's always a way through. We've got something we hadn't before—this story about a woman. And we know the fire was caused by phosphorus so conditioned that it burned slowly for a couple of hours inside a roll of clothes, and then got them going. The fire chief's report makes that certain."

"You can't get away from facts. They shouldn't have let a stranger in. Goddamighty, they can't even describe the face because of that damned veil!"

"We've got to take it both ways," Roger said. "Things go wrong nearly as often as they go right —but we usually get a break. We can't work miracles, but—"

"Miracles hell! Why—"

"Shut up!" Now Roger glowered. "We catch two out of three crooks, and that means we lose one out of every three. That's the way it goes. We're understaffed, and we always start in the dark. Get that into your head. We aren't given a nice set of rules to learn, we can't guess where to find the crooks, and we can't smell them, either. Stop squawking like a conceited lout, and—"

Turnbull said harshly: "Listen, West, no one's going to talk to me like that." His high color had gone, he was a creamy pallor, his eyes were glittering.

"I'll talk to you the way I think you need," Roger rasped.

Turnbull stood up slowly; a gigantic figure.

Roger sat where he was, at his desk, face set tightly, lips compressed. Turnbull just stood there, clenching his big hands. Two veins were beating in his neck, non-stop; and one was swelling in his temple.

This was crazy; two men in charge of the case, squabbling.

Crazy was one word.

"All right, forget it," Roger made himself say. "We know it's a woman or a man masquerading as a woman, which is more likely, and—"

Turnbull said through his teeth, "Now teach me my ABC. That's if you know yours. God, you make me sick! Sometimes I wonder if you want to see the end of this case. How you ever put anyone inside I don't know. You ought to be a ruddy wet-nurse to your kids, or a housemaid petting your wife. You dare talk to me as if I were—"

Roger said: "That's enough." He had to struggle to keep his voice steady. "We've a job on. When we've finished it we can fight if we want to." He held his whole body stiff.

Turnbull said: "No one's going to call me a conceited imbecile and get away with it."

"Lout was the word," Roger said. He wanted to get up, wanted to strike the other, nothing would have given him fiercer satisfaction than a fight. He sat where he was. "You can please yourself. We go on from where I stopped, or you get off the case."

Turnbull was breathing through distended nostrils.

"And I don't want to make trouble," Roger said. "Yet."

He fell silent again.

Turnbull's breathing was noisy; gusty; Roger could see the struggle that the man was putting up. He waited long enough, he hoped, and then looked down at his notes and went on:

"The man masquerading as a woman is much more likely. We know the clothes, the hat, and the shoes worn. There's another thing we know now even if we didn't before. You seen it?"

Would the explosion come now, or would it be repressed until later?

Turnbull muttered: "What?"

So it was postponed.

"The courage and cool nerve of the killer," Roger said flatly. "It's stop at nothing and kill at any cost. Is it just a lunatic attempt to get a favorite top of Conway's Competition? Could there be a secondary motive to that—killing for killing's sake, because the killer hates all beauty?"

The thought forced its way through Turnbull's vicious mood, even changed the expression in his eyes.

He said: "...who *hates* beauty?"

"That's it. The way some people love it. Regina Howard or any one of these girls would make most men lose their heads, given the time and place. See how Regina affected Osborn. Supposing we're up against someone who's affected the other way."

184

Turnbull said slowly, heavily, "It's conceivable, I suppose. How long have you been thinking that?"

"It's come and gone," Roger said. He was able to breathe more easily now; and the way out of this impasse had been to give Turnbull a new idea. "It could also be one beauty who hates all her rivals. One Queen," he added.

Turnbull dropped into his chair, partly from nervous reaction. When he lit a cigarette, it was with a savage motion.

"You mean—one of the Queens' hatred for the others. I—oh, hell!" He tossed the cigarette to the floor as the smell of Turkish tobacco began to creep about the room, and stamped on it savagely.

Roger said, "We've an outsize job on our hands, and if smoking those things helps you to concentrate, go ahead and smoke them."

"I can manage. Well, we're getting places. One of the Queens might be so insanely jealous of the others. Not someone who wants to see a particular girl win, but a Queen in person."

"That's it."

"It's a foul idea."

"It's just an idea. But remember two of them might be working this together, boy and girl. And also remember that a lot of men would lose their heads for a real beauty, would become so enslaved that whatever the lady said would be the right word. Oh, it could happen. If the woman's a Delilah, she could possess him body and soul, she'd blind him to everything else."

"You're talking about—Regina."

"And one other, remember—Norma Dearing."

"Oh, that milky piece couldn't make anyone's blood race, but Regina—" Turnbull snatched out

185

his gold case and lit another cigarette; Roger was quite sure that he didn't realize what he was doing. "Forget it. We're looking for a man. We're looking for Dickerson. Forgotten him? He's ready made."

"That's what I'm afraid of. Ready made—or put up to be knocked down."

"If he's dressing up as a woman it would explain why we haven't found him, wouldn't it?"

"Oh, it could be. Only we aren't taking anything for granted. I'm going to check on the two Queens," Roger went on. "I've got to make sure that neither of them was out during the night. I'm going alone, and I want you to stay and collect reports and go over everything we've got to see if you can get a glimmer of anything new."

That would be a test of the man's mood and strength of mind. They just sat and eyed each other, Turnbull breathing smoke through his distended nostrils.

It was almost comic.

He jumped up.

"All right," he grunted. "Call me when you've put the bracelets on them."

Roger grinned in spite of himself.

"I will. And our personal pride apart, we're on our mettle."

"Why?"

"Conway's are raising merry hell. It's costing them—"

He handed Turnbull a letter which Chatworth had received and passed on, showing how many tens of thousands of pounds Conway's estimated they were losing.

Turnbull glowered.

"Now I'm really worried," he sneered.

He went out, like the last blustering squall of a furious storm.

Roger groped for his cigarettes, lit one, and stared at the blue sky and the bright-green leaves and the little segment of Big Ben that he could see. He felt cold, in spite of the warmth, and he was shivery. He realized that both of them had been living on their nerves; that each jarred the other unbearably. But that flare-up had been close to real trouble, and he felt sure that it had only been postponed. Turnbull's reaction to the Conway prod had been characteristic, but Conway's angle was important to Conway's and to shareholders; and the combine could make a lot of unpleasantness for the Yard.

Roger finished his cigarette, then went downstairs to Chatworth's office. The A.C. was dictating to a secretary who wouldn't have won a beauty prize in the wilds of Africa. But she was good, and she went out the moment she recognized Roger.

"All right, all right," Chatworth said, "you're doing your best. I know it. It won't help to have the skin off the backs of the police in Wembley, either." He tried to rumble, but couldn't. "I take it there's no need to ask you if you've seen the *Globe* and the rest of the newspapers."

"The laugh's on the *Globe*, I hope their man gets fired," Roger said. "We're looking for Dickerson, and we simply can't find him."

"Sure it's Dickerson?"

"No," Roger said, "but everyone else seems to be, from the newspapers downward." He looked broodingly into Chatworth's eyes. "It's rubbing me

187

red raw. The first three were bad enough, but two since we've been aware of what's on—"

"Listen," said Chatworth, standing up. He looked rather like a gorilla trying to be friendly, and homespun tweeds made his paunch look mammoth. "We've had this kind of crime before, and unless we all get second sight we'll have it again. But don't let anything happen to the girls who are left."

"I want to take them away from their homes and hide them," Roger said. "Smuggle them away, make a big secret of it, and then let a rumor or so get out."

"Why?"

"There are moments when I think it's one of the girls, moments when I call myself crazy for even thinking it could be," Roger said. "Either or both might be next on the killer's list. Talbot's still a possibility. Dickerson might have an accomplice we don't even suspect. So if we hide the two Queens and let Talbot know where they are, we'll have a clearer idea about him."

"Using the girls as guinea pigs? I don't know that I like it."

"They'll be better protected with us."

Chatworth drew a deep breath.

"Oh, do it your way, but for Pete's sake don't let anything happen to them."

"Thanks, sir," Roger said. "Jim Fullerton's place out at Putney Heath would be about right, and he'll play. His wife's away, and won't be there this week." He stood up. "There's one other thing. Neither Osborn nor Talbot has alibis for each murder. They could be working together. Osborn's act at the cottage could be to fool us. We know it wasn't him last night, but—"

"Talking of Osborn," Chatworth interrupted, "I've just had a medical report from the high-ups. He's undoubtedly had a nervous breakdown, and will have to have a long course of treatment. The report is exhaustive, and the official opinion is that he's unlikely to be the killer. I never quite know how much to believe of what these know-alls tell us, but apparently Osborn lost his mother when he was five, and his father two years later. The medical mumbo jumbos say that's put the inhibition right in deep, he's afraid of losing anyone he loves. And his love for Regina Howard is possessive and passionate. Danger to her because of the murders sent him over the line."

Roger didn't speak.

"Well, do what you can with the job," Chatworth growled. "Oh, by the way—how's Turnbull?" He grinned unexpectedly. "Gnashing his teeth, by the look of him. Make him understand that things do go wrong sometimes, and you can't sweep through every case."

"I'm trying," Roger said.

"Is he still good?"

"Yes."

"Why the tone of reservation?"

"I think I'll know when we're through on this job," Roger said. "Anything else, sir?"

"No," rumbled Chatworth, "look after yourself."

Regina Howard just looked hopeless and pale when she heard about the latest murder.

She said that she'd slept better that night than for a long time, chiefly because she had taken two of the sleeping tablets prescribed for her mother. It seemed almost idiotic to think that she might be responsible for the murders. She raised no objection to the police making a search of her rooms and wardrobe; nothing was found to suggest that she had been out the night before. There were no scratches at the windows.

Roger checked with the night-duty men; none of them had seen or heard anything. Nor had those who had come on duty at six o'clock.

Roger drove from the Edgware Road to the Kentish suburb where the remaining Queen lived.

Norma Dearing was different from any of the other winners. Her parents, while not wealthy, were comfortably placed. They owned a large detached house standing in its own grounds overlooking a park. In the delightful garden, a gardener worked two days a week, and there was a living-in maid; comfort not far removed from luxury.

Norma was the true English type, fair-haired, blue-eyed, with an unbelievably perfect skin. She was likely to be dubbed Miss England wherever she competed, but she lacked one of the qualities which Barbara Kelworthy had possessed: vitality. Hers was a languid beauty, and her creamy skin and limpid eyes did nothing to excite—as Barbara had; as Regina did.

She was almost blasé.

"The only thing I can say, Chief Inspector, is that I'm surprised the police have been so unsuccessful, but I suppose I shall just have to put up with it until the beast *is* caught. I admit I'm frightened, but it's no use giving way to panic, is it, and I'm sure you're doing your best."

"Yes. Where were you last night, Miss Dearing?"

"Here, of course; if it wasn't for television, I'd be bored stiff. Earlier I had a game of tennis with my brother, that's all. But can't you ask the policemen who were *supposed* to be watching?"

Roger said, "Yes. Have you a light-gray suit?"

Norma stared. "Why, yes," she said, "as a matter of fact I have two. Why should that interest you?"

"I'd like to have a look at them, please," Roger said.

She didn't argue.

Her mother went upstairs with them; in all they had three light-gray suits between them, but none was of the plain serge the police had described as being worn by the veiled woman.

Roger checked everything as thoroughly as if the people here were major suspects, but with sinking hopes. This was the kind of thing they'd been doing from the beginning. It was simple routine, too; the girl would hardly have got away from this guarded house, with lawns surrounding it.

"Now that you've finished, Chief Inspector," Norma said, "I would be grateful if you could tell me what all this is about?"

Roger said, "It's a routine check, Miss Dearing." He watched her very closely. "Miss Kelworthy died last night."

The mother just dropped down onto a chair, and gasped, "Oh, dear God!"

The girl took it very well. Her creamy skin paled as some of the color receded, and her eyes took on an added sparkle as fear touched her. But she didn't shrink back, didn't show any signs of collapse, and her voice remained quite firm and clear.

"I suppose you have to check everything, but I didn't leave here last night. Do you—do you yet know who did it?"

"No."

"Have you found Mr. Dickerson?"

"No."

"Oh, Norma," her mother said brokenly, "there's only just the two of you left, just you and Regina Howard."

"I know," Norma said, in the same clear voice, "but please don't fuss, Mother. All the same, I would like to feel that nothing else can go wrong, Chief Inspector."

Roger had seldom admired a woman more.

"We'll do everything we can, but it's partly up to you, you know. I'd like you to leave here, after dark tonight, with me and several other C.I.D. men. We'll take you to a place where you can't be followed, no one will know where you are. We can't make you come, but—"

He broke off.

"All right," Norma decided promptly. "I'll do whatever you think best. Will Regina Howard be coming?"

"Yes, I think so."

"At least he won't be able to kill us both at the same moment," Norma said, dryly. "What time will you call?"

"Eleven o'clock," Roger said. He looked at her levelly, and as levelly at her mother. "Don't tell anyone outside the family that you're going."

"We won't," said Norma emphatically, "and if I don't know where I'm going I can't tell anyone that, can I?" She gave a queer little strangled laugh. "You'll come yourself, won't you? I couldn't bring myself to leave with strangers."

"I'll come myself," Roger promised.

20

Night Journey

Derek Talbot flicked a match away, and it struck the frame of the open window of the living room at Regina's house. It was nearly seven o'clock that evening. He had brought her from the office in a taxi, to find Roger West waiting for her. Her mother was still with neighbors.

"It's all right as far as it goes, Hawkshaw," Talbot said thinly, "but I don't really like the idea of Regina being spirited away from under my nose, as it were. After all, the police have fallen down badly on this, haven't they?"

Regina spoke quietly. "Derek, it's wise, and provided we can do it without worrying Mother, I'm quite happy."

"*Votre mère* can console herself with neighbors," Talbot said, almost nastily. "Do you understand me, West? You've been a very decent scout, but the same can't be said for everyone on the Force, including one I won't name. There's an old saw about setting a thief to catch a thief."

"Derek—" Regina began.

Roger smoothed down his curly hair. It wasn't easy to smile, but no occasion had ever called for more patience.

"I see what you mean. The one person who could fool us easily is a policeman."

"Precisely."

"Why don't you stop talking nonsense?" Regina demanded. "I can tell Mother that I've got to be away on business. Provided the Jamesons can put her up for a night or two, it'll be all right. When she's back, I'll go and see them. Can I telephone my answer?"

Roger said very quietly, "You'll come with me, Miss Howard, or you'll have to take the consequences."

"The police get uppish," Talbot sneered. "They can't stop it themselves, so they're finding ways and means of blaming the victims." He was looking impudently into Roger's eyes; then something in their expression made him change his tune. His eyes dropped. "All right, West. Sorry. I'm on edge, too. Couldn't be worse if I were on the killer's list myself."

"Derek," Regina said, "I think you'd better go."

He looked her up and down, and his eyes kindled. In spite of all that had happened, she was really magnificent to look at. In all this surfeit of beauty, hers would always have freshness.

"Yes, beloved," he said. "Yours obediently. But West had better not let anything happen to you. I hereby vow, if he does and you don't come back, that I shall render an account to him myself, personally, and with violence." His smile was very brittle. "I wonder if you'd spare a minute with me solo, so to speak."

195

Her eyes pleaded. "Derek, not now."

He shrugged. "All right, sweet. I'll make it a public confession. I love you." He blew her a kiss, but there was a wry twist at his lips. "No response from my Regina. I really am without hope, aren't I?"

"Please, Derek—"

He shrugged again, and turned away. Roger pretended to look at him, but actually watched the girl. There was a film of tears in her eyes. Her hands were clenched very tightly. It was hard to say whether she had any affection for Talbot, or whether she was just sorry for him. It was as difficult to judge whether she was badly frightened or not. There had been no doubt about Norma Dearing's fear, but now he wondered about Regina's.

Need he?

Talbot was halfway out of the room when he looked back.

"Postscript," he said with more effective lightness. "If the police lose the next Queen in this pretty game of chess, there'll only be one left. The winner!" He gave his wry smile again. "*Could* anyone have seriously expected to get away with it for you, Gina?"

She didn't answer.

He went out. The front door closed.

There was a curious tension in the room. Then the girl seemed to let herself go for the first time, and she buried her face in her hands and went blindly toward a chair. Roger didn't help her. She knocked the chair with her leg, then dropped into it. Her shoulders moved as she cried, but there was hardly a sound from her.

Roger stood watching.

196

At last, she looked up. Tears smeared her cheeks, and she made no attempt to wipe them away. She didn't try to smile or pretend to make light of her feelings.

"I've never felt so dreadful," she said. "It's as if I've got to kill or be killed." She looked at him straightly, and only the old tears were in her eyes, she wasn't crying now. "Will you look after me?"

"I don't think you need worry," Roger said gently, and tried hard to be convincing.

"Please," she began, and then broke off, stared out of the window, and gritted her teeth; he could hear the sound. "Please don't let Derek know where you're going to take me," she said. "I think —I think he frightens me. He always has, he's so ruthless. Am I being disloyal?" The question had the strength of great sincerity.

She need never know that Roger was lying.

"I won't tell him," he promised.

One of the difficulties was keeping the facts away from the Press. Public interest had never been higher in any contemporary case. The *Globe* had made it its own, and men from several other popular newspapers seemed to haunt the Yard. There was no law against that. There was no law against the fact that a Press man was nearly always to be seen at the end of Bell Street, watching Roger; one or two near Regina's house, others within sight of Norma Dearing's home. The Press was on the lookout everywhere. Sometimes that helped; as often as not it was a handicap.

There were ways and means of avoiding them which any Yard man could use. The important thing was not to let them know that they were being avoided. Although he wanted the "secret" to leak as far as Talbot, Roger didn't want it in the newspapers. To get Regina Howard and Norma Dearing away from their homes without newspapermen discovering it was going to need a lot of careful staff work.

The girls co-operated; so did the Dearing family. Mrs. Howard, still with the neighboring Jamesons, didn't know what was being planned.

The actual move was done swiftly and easily. An ordinary London taxi swung along the road and stopped outside Regina's house. She was ready. Two policemen went with her to the cab, and West leaned out of it to grip her hand and help her in. Two reporters, on the trail in a matter of seconds, were blocked at the end of the street.

An hour later, escorted by police cars in front and behind, the cab turned into the driveway of a large block of flats overlooking Putney Heath. It was then after midnight, and no one was about. Wearing a floppy hat which hid her face, Regina was hustled up to an apartment on the top floor.

Norma Dearing was already there.

Roger watched the meeting of the two girls closely. They had met casually before—at the competition when Norma had won her prize. There was a moment of hesitation. The English Rose of Norma was quite perfect, and excitement had given her more expression, greater vitality, but she was still reserved. The beauty of Regina was different, because everything she did and said was with such supreme naturalness.

After that momentary pause, while they eyed each other, Regina put out her hands. They

198

gripped; and Regina squeezed and drew the other girl to her, kissing her lightly on the cheek.

"It's good to see you, Norma. I do hope it isn't worrying you too much."

Norma said, "Well, it can't last much longer, anyhow." She seemed more reassured.

They moved about the flat, seeing the bars at the windows of two rooms, the special lock at each of the doors, the alarm system, and the guard system. Every window and every entrance to the block of flats was under constant surveillance; and flood-lighting, usually switched off after midnight, was still on, and would stay on until the hunt was over.

The girls had adjoining rooms.

Roger left them together, had a word with the man in charge of the precautions, Wiltshire of the Yard, and then went down in the lift. No new staff had been taken on, there were no new tenants, absolutely nothing at all to suggest that Dickerson or anyone else had entrée here.

Roger would spread the whisper about in a day or two, and intensify the watch on Talbot.

But the next move caught Roger by surprise.

A Chelsea policeman, on his ordinary afternoon patrol, saw a "woman" with Dickerson's face.

Roger sensed the constable's excitement, secretly sympathized, outwardly was poker-faced.

"I'm quite sure it was the wanted man's face, sir. Believe me I've studied that face for hours, my wife's fair sick of the way I've stuck at it." He had a slightly West Country burr. "I couldn't make a mistake, and there it was, but he was wearing a woman's suit. A light-gray suit, sir, I'm positive."

"Good, Harris, this is just what we needed to know. What did you do?"

"I didn't let on I'd recognized him," Harris said eagerly. "I walked past with a face as straight as yours is now, sir, and turned the corner before I did a thing. Had a bit of luck, there was Sergeant Dowse on his bike, so I tipped him the wink, and he rode off and phoned the Yard, sir. Thought it best to go straight to the Yard instead of through the Division. Maybe I was wrong, but—"

"Your Super will forgive you!" Roger reassured him.

They were already on the way to the house near the Thames at Chelsea, where the woman with Wilfrid Dickerson's face had been seen. It was the moment Roger had been waiting for; he felt an almost painful suspense. Harris was sure, but could have been mistaken; minutes should show.

The house, large, massive, and made of red brick, with an overgrown garden, a shrubbery where several men could hide, a double garage, and, at one corner, a slate-roofed tower, was surrounded by Yard men and Divisional police. The excitement touched every man, showed in eyes, in bearing. No car was very near, nothing was left to chance when Roger and the Divisional Superintendent went along the drive. The gravel was thick with thrusting weeds, everything had an air of neglect, but there were curtains at the window, and nothing to suggest that the house was empty.

They knocked and rang; there was no answer.

With a dozen police waiting and watching, tensely, Roger found a window open at the back, close to the garage. If Dickerson, or the "woman" like him had escaped, he could have hidden from the constable, walked behind the garage, and climbed into the next garden.

The two policemen went from room to room, landing to landing, passage to passage, feeling almost suffocated.

They didn't find Dickerson, but they found two gray serge suits, and a woman's underclothes, stockings, shoes which were large for a woman. Dickerson's fingerprints were everywhere. There were some fireworks and a few simple "joke" tricks, to make smoke and small explosions.

And in one room of the first floor there were seven large photographs, one of each Queen. They were in the form of show cards for Conway's soaps and toilet aids. Five stood with the faces to the wall, only Regina's and Norma's faces were showing.

Roger turned the others round.

Each had been slashed with red paint or with lipstick, a hideous disfigurement.

The faces of the two living girls were not touched.

Only one other "clue" was found—a visiting card, dusty and soiled, reading:

The Rev. A. Millsom,
St. Cleo's Vicarage,
Chelsea.

21

Message for Talbot

The Vicar of St. Cleo's, in his book-lined study, which had a lived-in, rather threadbare look, made no attempt to deny that he had known Dickerson. He still looked much older; as if the shock of what had happened to his son would never lose its hurt.

"Yes, I've known Wilfrid Dickerson for many years," he said. "He was once a parishioner of mine, here. We're not close friends, mind you, little more than acquaintances."

"Did he know your son?"

"Yes, he knew Harold," answered Millsom, quite steadily. "In fact, Harold once wanted to get a job at Conway's. Dickerson dissuaded him."

Almost automatically, because his mind was moving so fast, Roger asked, "Why?"

"He didn't think that a large combine of that kind would give Harold full scope. He was rather —resentful, you know."

Roger said more sharply, "Resentful of what?"

"His position with Conway's."

"Do you know why?"

"Oh, yes," answered the clergyman, "and in a way it's difficult to blame him. He once had a small soap-manufacturing business which he inherited from his father. Conway's made competition too fierce, and forced him out of business. Actually, his little firm was absorbed, and he was given a salaried post in the combine. It was reasonable compensation, I think, but—"

The clergyman stopped, as if he couldn't see that this would be of any interest to the police.

"How long ago was this?" asked Roger.

"It must be over thirty years."

"Did you know Mrs. Howard?"

"No," said Millsom. "I knew that Dickerson was unfortunate in a love affair, but only since I've been reading about the case in the newspapers did I know who the woman was." The priest leaned back in a leather armchair, the arms of which were badly worn, and closed his eyes. He looked very tired. "I have been trying to make up my mind to come and see you all day, Mr. West, but couldn't be quite sure that it was necessary."

Roger, fully relaxed, said, "You'd be surprised how little things can help."

"Yes. It's about the poison. The arsenic."

Roger sat up. *"What?"*

Millsom opened his eyes. There was the familiar strange calmness in them—as if he were still fighting back emotions which he knew he should not have.

"I've read about the poisoned chocolates, of course, and the search for weed-killer. Only this morning I found a tin missing from my greenhouse." He anticipated the next question, and went on very deliberately: "The last time I used it was a few days before my son came here."

His voice was very low-pitched, almost empty, as if he were touched by deep despair.

Turnbull said briskly, "Well, we got a bit out of the parson after all. You say he still says he can't tell us any more about why his son cut and run?"

"That's what he says."

"He's probably lying," Turnbull said carelessly. "But he's given us something, and how! We've got the name of the weed-killer, know that Dickerson could have lifted it, know that Dickerson knew the church, including the steeple, that he and young Millsom might have met at the vicarage, working together in this. I know, I know, half of that will have to be washed out, but it's still plenty."

"See anything else?" Roger asked.

"In what?"

Roger said mildly, "In the report." He'd made it out comprehensively, and Turnbull had read and studied a copy.

Turnbull looked at him almost suspiciously.

"No. Is there anything?"

"I don't know. Think over it; if the same idea strikes you we might have some answers." He offered Turnbull a Virginian cigarette, and Turnbull took it and grinned. But he was puzzled.

"If there's anything else in that report, I'll squeeze it out," he said. "Thanks. Anything on Talbot?"

"Not yet," Roger said. "But there's time."

*   *   *

Derek Talbot got out of bed on the second morning after Regina had been taken away by the police, and sat with his chin on his hands, looking moodily at the window. Unshaven, hair disheveled, pale-blue pajamas rumpled, he was nothing like the exquisite who made such an impression on so many people.

He grunted and stood up, made himself some tea, then went to the front door. The newspaper had just been pushed through the letter box, and the post hadn't arrived. It was just after seven o'clock, and he was as tired as he looked. He had slept fitfully; he had been sleeping fitfully for a long time.

He opened the *Globe*. The headline cried:

DICKERSON HIDEOUT FOUND

Talbot felt his heart lurch, actually had to steady himself against the wall. He read intently, all tiredness fading. The whole story was there, how the policeman had seen the "woman with Dickerson's face," how the police had raided the house, what they had found; and across the foot of the front page were reproductions of the photographs of the seven Queens. All but two of them were slashed. "As if with blood," gloated the *Globe*.

Talbot made his tea. . . .

As he shaved and ran the water for his bath, he could see little in his mind's eyes except the photograph of Regina; and Regina herself. His face was taut, lined, much older than his years. He did everything slowly and deliberately. When stripped, the muscles at his back, shoulders, and arms rippled easily, there was lean and wiry strength in him; and yet everything he did suggested that he was very tired.

He toweled slowly, then dressed with his usual care.

Nothing would make him hurry. The *Globe*, open at the front page, was spread out on his dressing table; as if it exerted some unholy fascination.

There were sounds at the front door; the post.

He went to get it. Two or three bills he tossed aside; a letter from a friend who was in France he opened and scanned. The other letter was addressed in block lettering, and that didn't really surprise him. Many people wanting favors for the Conway's Competition found out his private address, and all kinds of illiterate scribbles reached him, as well as some of the smoothest begging letters he could hope to see.

He opened this one.

She's with the other girl at 28 Hill Crest Court, Putney Heath. Top flat, second building. If you want to save her life you'd better get her away, *I* know the way in.

The undercurrents of tension and dislike between Roger and Turnbull grew stronger not weaker; each man was aware of them, each was deliberately trying to ignore them. The discovery at Hampstead and the instant quickening of the hunt for Dickerson had buried the currents deep, but there had been days of inaction since.

Turnbull had seen nothing more in Roger's report.

The two girls were still at Putney. The rumors had been spread, cautiously, but there were moments when Roger told himself that to expect anyone to be fool enough to raid the apartment, knowing that the police were watching in strength, was asking for the moon.

At others, he was sure the attempt would be made.

Turnbull didn't commit himself to an opinion.

Turnbull was out, Roger at his desk, when the telephone rang just after nine-thirty, three mornings after they'd found Dickerson's hideout. The jarring note of the bell might mean anything. Roger snatched up the receiver.

"West."

"Will you speak to Mr. Derek Talbot?"

"Put him through," Roger said, and a moment later, "Good morning, Mr. Talbot."

"West, I must see you," Talbot said abruptly. "I'd rather not come to the Yard, and I don't want anyone to see us."

"What's it about?"

"I've had a letter from Dickerson," Talbot said. "Anyhow, I think it's Dickerson."

Roger didn't waste time.

"Leave your flat, go to Piccadilly Circus, and wait by Swan & Edgars. A green Morris will slow down just there. Nip inside, and the driver will see that you shake off anyone who's following."

"Will I recognize the driver?"

"Probably," Roger said dryly.

Half an hour later, he pulled up opposite Eros in the gilded cage, and saw Talbot staring along Piccadilly. A policeman moved toward the driver who

207

had dared to stop where traffic should go in perpetual motion.

Roger waved him away, and walked swiftly along.

"Hallo, Talbot."

Talbot started violently. "Lord, you scared me!" He looked round nervously. "I'm full of the heebie-jeebies, shadows follow me all over the place. Where's your outsize Romeo?"

They hurried to the car. Roger saw a Yard man, doubtless the one who was on Talbot's tail. The man recognized him and gave an almost imperceptible signal.

No one else was following.

"Why do you want to see me?" asked Roger, driving off.

Talbot struck a theatrical gesture; he was trying very hard to be flippant.

"Hi, Super Sleuth with his nose to the trail! I have a Mysterious Missive. I telephoned you because I wanted to talk to you about it, and from now on I will not deal with Copper Nob the Copper's Don Juan. Unless there's any special reason, I shall not see your Turnbull again. I hate the sight and sound of him. I don't even believe he would be good for Regina. Is it part of a policeman's job to trifle with the affections of a woman in a case?"

Roger said, "Talbot, I've a lot to do."

"I am about to disgorge the secret. But I lured you out in order to make one or two simple statements of fact that I can't make at Scotland Yard or within the hearing of the newspaper hounds. I think Turnbull's a clot and a swine. Is he serious with Gina?"

"I'm not Turnbull's keeper."

208

"You're his senior at the Yard, and you ought to keep him on a leash," Talbot flashed. "If he's fallen for Gina in a big way, well that's my cue to set out for Australia or far, far away. I might even wish them good luck from a distance. But if he's fooling around with her just to try to get the answer to this murderous business, then I'd—" Talbot broke off, and gripped his own coat lapels so tightly that the knuckles showed white. "Come across, West. Is Turnbull leading Gina up the garden as part of his copper's job?"

Roger said quietly, "Turnbull's had no instructions to work that way, it certainly wouldn't have official sanction, and as far as I'm concerned Turnbull's running big risks in seeing so much of Miss Howard."

"Well, that's a gust of refreshing frankness," Talbot said, as if surprised. "Thanks. What kind of risks?"

"He could be prejudicing an important witness," Roger said. "He's laying himself wide open to attack from the Press. If you want my private opinion, he's making a ruddy fool of himself because he can't help it. If you ever say that to him or to anyone else—"

"Oh, Hawk-eye! Grant me some honor. Thanks, anyway." Talbot took a letter from his pocket. "Here's the real reason I want to see you. I've a nasty feeling that I'm being watched all the time and didn't want to be seen passing this over." He handed over the letter, and Roger turned into Whitehall and pulled up.

"You see the nasty cunning of it, I trust," Talbot went on. "I got the letter. So I, Sir Galahad the Second, go to rescue my Queen Regina. I get nabbed. The police are meant to reason, 'Ah-ha, he's discovered where the lovelies are and is going to make another kill.' Only I am not a killer, as you may guess."

Roger had read the message twice.

"When did you get this?"

"This morning, at about seven fifty-one."

"Do you recognize the writing?"

"No."

"I see," Roger said. "Thanks, Talbot, I'm glad you didn't lose any time."

This did not mean beyond doubt that Talbot was in the clear; Talbot could have written the letter and posted it to himself. It had a West Central postmark. But he wouldn't have, had he wanted to make a secret visit to the two girls; and would a guilty man make sure that the authorities knew that someone had the girls' address, and so put them on their guard?

Talbot almost sneered. "Don't miss the other obvious clue, will you? Killer Boy knows where the two Queens are, Killer Boy might have another trick up his sleeve. Get Gina away from that place, West." The last sentence spat out. "Understand? It's not safe for her there."

"We'll look after her."

"As you did sweet Barbara Kelworthy!"

After a long pause, Roger said quietly, "Talbot, take my tip and get some rest. You don't look as if you've had much lately. If you get any more messages, let me know at once—telephone and tell me next time. If you prefer not to come to the Yard, we'll meet outside again."

"The fatherly policeman," Talbot mocked. "All right. I'll be good. Only one spot where I can get any peace, these days; ever heard of the halt lead-ing the blind? If you want me, I'll be at Regina's place."

Roger said, "Don't go making it worse for Mrs. Howard."

"We comfort each other," Talbot said. "Odd, isn't it?"

He shivered.

"Where shall I drop you?" Roger asked.

"Oh, anywhere."

Roger chose a spot in Whitehall Place. The Yard sergeant had kept up with them—and so had someone else, who had done a remarkable job of shadowing.

Turnbull also followed Talbot.

Roger drove back to the Yard.

Roger was back in his office after a snack lunch, by half-past two. The first thing he got was a message from the Yard sergeant—Talbot had slipped him. Did it matter? It was easy to give your man the slip, no matter how good he was, but Talbot may have done it accidentally. He probably meant to go to Regina's home.

The sergeant was coming back, and could check.

There were half a dozen reports, but none from Turnbull, who had not even taken the trouble to telephone a report. He was behaving as if he was answerable to no one, and before long Chatworth would explode.

The telephone bell rang.

It might be a routine call, it might be dynamite. That was the kind of tension Roger felt.

"Mr. West," said the girl operator, in a tone which told him it wasn't routine, "I've had a call

211

from Paddington. The Station Inspector just left a message—would you go to the Howards' home at once? Mr. Derek Talbot's been attacked there, and they are afraid that he's dying."

22

To Live or To Die?

As Roger pulled up just behind the ambulance outside Regina's house, they were carrying Talbot out. It was a poignant reminder of when the boys had been poisoned.

A crowd had gathered, and the police were being severe. Roger pushed his way through.

Talbot's face was just visible; very pale, with the bags under his eyes looking almost black. His head was a massed turban of white bandages, but the bright crimson of blood was showing through in places.

The Divisional police surgeon was there.

"Will he live?" Roger asked, tautly.

"Fifty-fifty."

"You going with him?"

"No, nothing more I can do. He'll be on the table within an hour. His big chance is that Phillipson is at the hospital today; if anyone can save him, Phillipson can."

"So it's the head?"

"Battered something dreadful," the doctor said.

"As if someone just bashed for the sake of bashing." He was a hardened campaigner of forty disillusioning years, there was little he hadn't seen in the way of brutal savagery; but he was shaken. "Either someone went mad, or the assailant wanted to pretend he was crazy."

The ambulance doors closed, and Talbot was driven off. Roger and the police surgeon went into the little house.

"Where's Mrs. Howard?"

"Three or four doors along. She ran out of the house, screaming, that's what raised the alarm."

Roger nodded.

They went into Regina's bedroom, and there was no need to be told that this was where the attack had been made. A pale-colored tiled fireplace was smothered in blood, especially at one corner. So was the surround. The carpet was damp and red with blood, too. The furniture had been pushed about in all directions, a glass vase was broken. The bedclothes were rumpled, although the bedspread was over it; someone had lain down there, as if to relax.

There was a familiar smell that Roger didn't like. Turnbull's Turkish tobacco?

"Obviously been a fight," the police surgeon said.

"Yes." Roger's eyes were roving; he felt as badly as he had ever felt. Men were taking measurements, and a photographer came in. "Find anything?"

"This," the police surgeon said.

It was a half-smoked cigarette, which explained the familiar smell. The cork tip was still damp, and the gilt lettering on the stub was plain: Half Moon Turkish.

"I'll take that," Roger said. "Thanks." He put it in an envelope. "Any ideas?"

"D'you mean guesses?"

"Your guesses are as good as most people's ideas," Roger said.

The police surgeon put his head on one side, and grinned.

"That's more like you! Haven't been yourself this morning—bit pale about the gills, too. Harassing business, of course, but it won't do anyone any good if you knock yourself out."

"Those guesses," urged Roger.

"Oh, all right! Someone just held Talbot's head in his hands and smashed it down on that corner. The position of the body, the actual position and nature of the wounds, all point that way. It wasn't an attack from behind. He was lying on his back. What's more, there were bruises on his cheeks—about there." The police surgeon pointed to his own cheekbones, and Roger had a vivid mind picture of someone holding Talbot's head in his hands. The thumb marks would be just about where the bruises were on Talbot's face. "Let's say he fell and knocked himself out on that corner," the police surgeon went on, "or else was dazed. The assailant just bent over him, grabbed his head, and—well, that was that. Bleeding was copious from nose and head. Didn't take long. Must have been hell."

"Anything else?" Roger's voice was brittle.

"No. Can't be sure how long he was lying there, but it wasn't very long. Blood was just beginning to get a surface film on it. The window was open, and there's quite a draft. The neighbors are out, no one seems to have heard anything."

Roger's gaze wouldn't settle, but kept roving. He came back to the pale tiles and the blood—and then he stiffened and moved forward, obviously not thinking of what the police surgeon was saying. He knelt down in front of the fireplace. There were bloodstains—but they weren't so haphazard as most of the others, there was a kind of form to them.

"Doc, come here."

The police surgeon was just behind him, breathing down his neck. A local policeman was standing, staring.

"What do you make of that?"

"Writing!" exclaimed the police surgeon. "His right hand was covered in blood, too. What's it say?" He pressed forward. The writing was two inches high, the letters were badly formed, but once one saw what they were, quite readable.

"The killer is—"

The last word, the name, had been rubbed out.

The killer had been named, and had come and wiped across the name, to smear it so that no one could ever hope to read what it was.

Roger said slowly, "I didn't know Talbot had any idea." He went to the telephone by Regina's bed. "This been tested for prints?"

The local man said, "Yessir."

"Thanks." Roger dialed the Yard, asked for Chatworth, was quickly put through. "I haven't much time, sir, but I wonder if you'll talk to Paddington Hospital, and find out if Mr. Phillipson, the surgeon operating on Derek Talbot—"

"On *whom?*"

216

"Yes, Derek Talbot," Roger repeated. "Find out if he needs any help. Talbot might live, but might die, and he seems to know the killer. Even if we could bring him round for a few seconds, just time enough to name the swine, it would do."

"Yes," Chatworth said. There were times when he was the most understanding man in the world. "All right. Report again when you can."

"Thank you, sir," Roger said stonily. He rang off, and went to look at the writing in blood, and muttered almost to himself, "There's blood on Talbot's sleeve. He could have rubbed it off himself, after collapsing again."

"You know, West," said the police surgeon, "if you were a patient of mine I'd say that you ought to go off duty and take at least a week's rest. At once. What the hell's the matter with you?"

"Sorry," Roger said. "I wasn't listening. Save Talbot if it's humanly possible, won't you?" He forced a smile. "Of course you will!"

He turned away and hurried out of the house.

The police surgeon and the local policeman stared after him.

He sat at the wheel of his car for a few seconds, smoking, and with the half-smoked Turkish cigarette in his hand. He was conscious of people staring at him. Two reporters came near—and went off. Then a woman came out of a house a little way along; he'd seen her before, and recognized her as Mrs. Jameson, the neighbor who was such a good friend of Mrs. Howard.

She came up to the car.

"It *is* Chief Inspector West, isn't it?"

"Yes." He forced a smile.

"I thought it was. Inspector, can you assure me

that Regina's all right? I can't let Mrs. Howard go back to the house, but she's almost hysterical for fear that Regina might have been hurt. She saw the man—"

"She needn't worry," Roger said. This jolted him out of contemplation of the Turkish cigarette. "Regina's quite safe."

"Would you—would you come and have a word with Mrs. Howard?"

What else was there to do?

He went into the neighbor's house. Mrs. Howard was walking round and round a small front room, her eyes feverishly bright, her lips looking bluish in a sharp reminder of the heart affliction. The one side of her face was like marble, the other twitching. She stopped abruptly when she saw him—and he was surprised that she recognized him so quickly.

"Mrs. Howard, I can give you my word that Regina is perfectly well," Roger said. "I've actually talked to her this morning. There's been a burglary at your house, and my men are in possession, but it's nothing to do with Regina, and as far as I can find nothing has been stolen. Unless you had a lot of money there."

"Money?" echoed Mrs. Howard. "It doesn't matter about money! I—"

She stopped, abruptly, waved her arms, and almost fell. Her eyes closed. The neighbor held her; hastily Roger grabbed her, too. Mrs. Howard's right hand fumbled at a small cloth bag tied to her waist. The neighbor snatched her hand away, opened the bag, and took out a small bottle, opened the bottle and shook a small brown tablet out onto her palm, then forced this into Mrs. Howard's mouth.

They stood back.

"I'll send for her doctor," the neighbor said worriedly, "but I think she'll be all right. Those pills work miracles with her. Thank you—thank you very much for coming."

"I'm glad you caught me," Roger said mechanically.

He went back to the car, got in, and drove off as two newspapermen bore down on him. He had no time for the Press; little time for anyone. The half-smoked Turkish cigarette was still in his pocket, as if it were burning him. He remembered the way Turnbull's eyes clouded as with rage and fury; he remembered how Turnbull hated Derek Talbot. He remembered how, only a few days ago, Turnbull had flung himself at Mark Osborn, and battered the man savagely.

There wasn't much doubt that Regina had the same effect on Turnbull as she had on Talbot and on Osborn.

Facts were facts, no matter how ugly.

Turnbull had followed Talbot, and Turnbull had been in the room.

Roger knew that he ought to report at once to the Yard and have a call put out for Turnbull, get him in, question him. There would be blood on the clothes and the hands of the attacker.

Turnbull had a bachelor's flat in Kensington.

Roger turned his car toward Kensington. His heart beat with a painful heaviness. Talbot lay between life and death, at least one person knew where to find Regina and Norma, Dickerson was still at liberty, and Turnbull—

He reached an old-fashioned building which had been converted into flats, and found Turnbull's name printed in black on a brown-polished board.

Detective Inspector Warren Turnbull, D.S.O., M.C.

It was like putting one's decorations on a private letter heading. Roger knew that Turnbull had won the awards, and it didn't surprise him. The man's physical courage couldn't be surpassed. But courage was largely a matter of sensitivity.

He walked up the stairs toward the first floor and the flat. Turnbull's name was on a small brass plate, complete with the D.S.O. and the M.C.

He rang the bell.

Now that he was here, he knew that he should never have come. He should have told Chatworth and left Chatworth to handle the situation. He hadn't done so because of the time when Turnbull had hung down from a narrow plank and held on to him, saving his life. A gunman had lurked there, too, and Turnbull hadn't given that a moment's thought.

Unless he had *known* that he was safe.

Roger rang the bell again.

There were movements, footsteps, a closing door; and then Turnbull opened his door.

23

Evidence

Turnbull wore a dressing gown, silk, shiny, a dazzling design of golds and blues. He looked enormous in it. His eyes were narrowed, but nothing could hide their tiredness. He was astounded at sight of Roger, and stood with his hands raised almost as high as his chest, mouth open a little.

Roger said, "Hallo. I want a talk."

He stepped forward. For a moment, he thought that Turnbull would stop him; but Turnbull let him pass, then slammed the door. That sounded very loud; it was like the slamming of a door in a deadly trap.

There was a hall and a bright front room overlooking some gardens. The sun was breaking through misty clouds. Roger couldn't have cared less about the room, yet could not fail to see that it was the room a rich man might possess. A big-screen, expensive television set was in one corner, and books lined the fireplace walls from floor to ceiling; expensive-looking books.

There was a baby grand piano, and on it a photograph of Regina Howard.

Turnbull said, "Look at me, not her. What do you want?"

"Have you given up working?" Roger asked brusquely.

"Hell, no, but wouldn't you like me to! I came home to change."

"You mean you came home to wash the blood off your hands," Roger said very softly.

Turnbull didn't speak, but his eyes seemed to grow huge and to flame.

"And your clothes." Roger made himself speak in a low voice, and stood absolutely rigid. "You murderous brute."

Turnbull's hands were still raised and clenched. Roger was big, Turnbull was bigger; and he began to breathe hissingly through his nostrils, the way he always did when he was fighting to keep his temper.

"Why attack Talbot?" Roger asked. He knew that there was no time for asking questions, but questions had to come out, he had to make Turnbull talk. "Why go there and do it? God, I don't understand what got into you."

"Talbot's the killer," Turnbull said. "And you were pretty close with him this morning. Nice and snug. I *saw* you. Conspiring with a killer—"

"Don't be a bloody fool!"

"So I'm a fool. That's right. A conceited lout, remember?" The words must have burned themselves into Turnbull's mind. "But *I* wasn't doing any deal with Talbot—how much did he pay you?"

Roger said, "Listen, Turnbull, you're a bigger fool than I thought."

"So I'm a fool," Turnbull repeated. His whole body began to tremble. "Get out, West. Get out of my flat before I break your neck." He caught his breath and then bellowed, "Get out, I tell you!"

"I'm on my way," Roger said. "But why kill Talbot?"

"The way you lie," sneered Turnbull. "Can't you dream up a motive like you dream up everything else?" So he was going to use flat denial; perhaps he was so full of conceit that he believed he could get away with it.

"I'll dream plenty up," Roger rasped. "You're in love with Regina. You know that she's the killer. So did Talbot, and he was going to talk. So—"

Turnbull leaped at him.

Roger was ready; he saw the great body move and he felt the wind of the sweeping blow, but swerved to avoid it. Everything he possessed was in the punch he smashed at Turnbull's chin; the timing was perfect, and Turnbull was moving into it. He just rocked back on his heels, then fell flat.

He didn't get up.

Roger turned slowly away from him, because a new sound intruded. He couldn't be sure that he knew everything, it was just possible, that was all. The ugly thing was that it made Regina guilty. Her beauty, her naturalness, her charm, all seemed to scream a denial.

Damn that sound, of a ringing bell, a—telephone, of course!

It was by the window. He had to step past Turnbull, whose eyes were open but glazed.

"This is Detective Inspector Turnbull's flat."

"Turnbull?" The voice, incredibly, was gruff and familiar; there couldn't be two voices like it, could there? Chatworth's. "Turnbull," Chatworth repeated, "is that you?"

Roger said, "West speaking, sir."

"Roger!" That was like an explosion, followed by a hissing pause. Then, "Listen, hold Turnbull, but be careful with him. He was seen leaving the Howards' house, half an hour before Talbot was found there. Be careful, mind you, he's an ugly customer when roused. Don't let him get away. He—"

"He's stretched out unconscious," Roger said. "He won't give any more trouble. Send someone, sir."

He rang off before Chatworth could comment.

It brought a curious feeling of relief. He'd given Turnbull a chance to explain, and the man hadn't taken it. Someone else had put the call out for him, others had seen him at the Howards' house, there was no need for him, Roger West, to lay the charge or start the hunt.

Keeping an eye on Turnbull, who was beginning to stir, Roger looked into the bedroom. It was luxurious, and had a large double bed. By the side of the bed was another picture of Regina, looking at her loveliest. On a chair was a crumpled brown suit.

There were bloodstains on the coat and the trousers.

Chatworth was bulkier and burlier than ever as he squatted on the corner of Roger's desk. Eddie Day and two other Chief Inspectors were in the room and so silent that it was hard to realize they were present. Chatworth might suddenly sweep out of the room and take Roger with him; and deny them the privilege of this.

It was nearly ten o'clock that night.

"...and I don't give a hoot what you think, you were wrong both ways. You should have taken someone else with you, knowing he was dangerous, if only to protect yourself. And believing what you did, you should have reported to me before you went to see Turnbull. You must be nearly as crazy as he is. And it's no use telling me that he once saved your life. This is a Criminal Investigation Department, not a Bureau for Sentimental Slops."

Roger took all this poker-faced.

Chatworth almost bit through a cheroot.

"All right, all right," he growled. "I know what you did it for, but if you ever take a chance like that again I'll—well, don't. Now, what's the position? Talbot's still unconscious. They may save his life, but he won't be able to talk for days. There's this theory that Regina Howard is the killer, perhaps working with Dickerson. That right?"

Roger said, "I don't rate it as high as a theory. I can only tell you what possibilities there are. It could explain why Turnbull attacked Talbot—there's no doubt that Turnbull is passionately in love with Regina Howard. And yet—"

"Well, don't hold out on us."

"It doesn't square up," Roger said abruptly. "At first I accepted it, but it can't be right. Turnbull hasn't made a statement, has he?"

"No. He sits in his cell like a betrayed bull. He didn't condescend to reply to the charge—which I made myself."

Roger said, "Would he take Talbot's head between his hands and kill and splash blood all over the place? Could a man with his training and his

225

flashes of brilliance make an elementary mistake like that? He'd know he would be caught. He might lose his temper and attack Talbot, but he wouldn't just batter him like that. That would make him a demon. It would mean he is witless, too, and he isn't. Above everything else, he's a detective. That's his dominating pride." Roger jumped up and pushed his chair back, then began to pace the room. "I can't believe that he'd let anything stop him from making an arrest. If he was sure Regina Howard was guilty he'd charge her, no matter what he felt toward her. I can see him smashing at Talbot, yes, but I just can't go any further."

Chatworth still perched on the desk.

"I see what you mean," he said. "Complete reversal of a personality. Too strong-willed to act out of character like that. But damn it—bloodstained clothes, dried blood found in his fingernails, a bloodstain smearing his right forearm—"

"I know," Roger said. "I still boggle at it. And I'd like to know if anyone who could have been Dickerson was near the Howards' house today. Because if Turnbull knocked Talbot out and then left him, someone else could have come along and finished him off. The one thing we can take for granted is that Turnbull isn't the killer—yet Talbot thought he could name the killer. We didn't worry about the Howards' house once Regina was away, that was the mistake." He was still pacing the room, keeping his voice low, and trying to pierce the mist which had enshrouded the case from the beginning. "We know Turnbull was there, but someone else might—"

He broke off.

Chatworth, knowing him, kept absolutely silent; so did the others.

Roger said softly, "There was one witness we haven't worried much, because we're scared of what might happen to her if she were high-pressured. Mrs. Howard. She ran screaming from the house, remember, that's how it was all discovered. Then she collapsed, and I couldn't question her. We haven't tackled her beyond formal questioning. I think we'll try again, sir." He was already looking more alert, his eyes were less shadowy, his face less drawn. And they knew he hadn't said everything he had in mind. "There's that old family friendship between her and Dickerson, too. She might be keeping quiet for old time's sake. She'll pay for questioning. I think I'll go over at once, but we'll need to check with her doctor that she can stand it. If necessary I think we ought to insist, and give the doctor—a woman—an opportunity to be present if she wants to be."

Chatworth was almost humble.

"All right, Roger, I'll see to that."

"Thanks," said Roger. He picked his hat off the stand. "I'll wait until I've word from you, sir."

He went out and downstairs. A youthful sergeant was waiting by the side of his car, warned to stand by. Roger spoke to him absently, then took the wheel. The night was cool, but the stars were out. There was little traffic, and he took the main roads, turned out of Oxford Street toward the Edgware Road, and was soon pulling up outside Regina's house.

He walked to it. The police now on duty saluted. He was there for ten minutes before Chatworth telephoned to say that the woman doctor would soon be at the neighbor's house.

Roger waited outside for her.

She was elderly, wary, but co-operative, and she knew the neighbor well.

"How is Mrs. Howard, Mrs. Jameson?"

"Well, she's asleep," the neighbor said. "I hate the thought of disturbing her. But if you say it's all right, Doctor..."

"We'll be gentle," promised the doctor. "Let me see, this is the room, isn't it?"

She opened a door.

She stepped inside, then stopped abruptly, causing Roger to bump into her. The exclamation at her lips and the sudden halt brought fear pounding into Roger's mind. He pushed past the doctor.

The room was empty; a window leading into the street was open.

Roger went into the street, told the police there to put out a general call for Mrs. Howard, then returned to the house.

24

The Killer

"Oh, dear," said the neighbor, gray hair misty against the open window. "She does worry me so much. She knows she shouldn't go out alone, and will *slip* away. I'm afraid—"

"Does she often go off without saying a word?" Roger rapped.

"Well, she has several times lately," said the neighbor. "I was so worried a few nights ago, but I didn't like to say anything to Gina about it, I know how she worries over her mother. It's too bad."

Roger said stonily, "What night were you so worried?"

"Well—" The neighbor waved her hands about. "It's difficult to be sure, but—"

It was as difficult to be patient, and it took half an hour to establish that on the night of the murder of Barbara Kelworthy, Mrs. Howard had been out until very late. She had been very ill next morning, but no one had been surprised, because she nearly always had a bad attack after her outings; the doctor's pills pulled her round, said Mrs. Jameson.

"One day she'll overdo it," the doctor said. "I've warned her time and time again. D'you mean you've no idea at all where she's gone?"

"Well, no," said the neighbor. "Except that—" She broke off, and gave a crackly little laugh. "It's so hard to say it about a woman in her fifties; if she were twenty years or so younger I'd say that she was going out to see her young man. As it is—"

Roger's voice was brittle.

"Is there a man friend?"

"Well, yes, there is," said the neighbor, and looked as if she wished she'd never broached the subject. "Mrs. Howard didn't want Gina to know, I think she felt rather embarrassed about it, and as I'd always understood that she hadn't much longer to live, I didn't see why I should worry her, so I kept her secret."

"Do you know the man?"

"Well—" The neighbor gulped, and something of Roger's tension touched her. "I do and I don't; he's a nice old man, and I think he has a little flat in Nettle Street. That's two streets away. An old-fashioned man, really, he dresses fifty years behind the times and has a beard, but he's sprightly enough. After all, it *is* her life, she can do what she likes with it, can't she?"

"Up to a point," Roger agreed. "Excuse me."

He went out of the house on the double, heart thudding.

The flat at 22 Nettle Street was located half an hour afterward. It was empty. Ten minutes' search proved that Dickerson's fingerprints were all over

230

the place; so he'd had several haunts. There was also a woman's light-gray suit, bundled up and thrust under a bed, and thick with bloodstains, as well as a small felt hat with a veil.

Descriptions of Dickerson dressed like a man of the 1900s, and of Mrs. Howard, were flashed to all London districts. That was at eleven twenty-one. By half-past, Roger was on his way to the Yard, with his walkie-talkie switched on.

A flash came from Information.

"Calling Chief Inspector West—Calling Chief Inspector West. A man describing himself as Wilfrid Dickerson is at the Putney Police Station, please proceed there at once. Calling Chief Inspector West—"

"Putney!" Roger burst out, and wrenched the wheel.

Dickerson might have stepped out of the pages of a *Tailor & Cutter* of 1901. He was small, gray, lined, nervous—and yet emphatic.

"I had to come and see you, because I'm afraid Maude will attack her own daughter," he said. "I'm afraid she kills for the sake of killing, now; when she got away with the first three, it did something to her. She was with me tonight, and then she ran away. I know she was coming this way, and she knew Regina's address, too. Also that other girl's. You see, she *hates* beauty—because her face was so disfigured when she had that crash. I've tried to reason with her, to help her, but I couldn't bear it if Regina were to suffer. Poor Regina..."

Roger growled, "Let's have the truth, Dickerson. You've been in this from the beginning. You've worked with Mrs. Howard."

"No," denied Dickerson in a strangely deliberate way. "I have tried to stop her. Not until I found her at the Chelsea house, with all those photographs, the poison, and—"

He broke off.

Roger didn't force the questions then. There was plenty of time. It would be better if Dickerson felt sure he was being believed.

"Does Regina know?" demanded Roger.

"About her mother being the killer? Oh, I don't think so," said Dickerson. "Of course I can't be sure, but I should be very surprised indeed. You see, Maude is very quiet and kind, usually; it's only when she thinks of what happened to her, and. . . ."

The moon was out, and the night was cool but pleasant. The leaves of the trees rustled in the grounds of the flat and on the Heath just across the road; the wind whispered through the grass and the shrubs, touching the curtains at the open window. There were lights at most windows and music from some of the rooms. Traffic passed by, headlights on, sweeping toward London or toward Kingston and the West.

The police, at their stations, hardly moved.

As Roger walked toward the entrance hall of Hill Crest Court, a shadowy figure emerged from one side.

"Mr. West—"

"Yes."

"No one's arrived, sir."

"All right. If Mrs. Howard comes, let her use the lift—and telephone me that she's on her way."

"Very good, sir."

The metal lift was small and self-operated. It

rose slowly. Roger looked out of the tiny window at each landing, and saw nothing. It came to a standstill gently, and he stepped out. A policeman appeared a moment later, from a hiding place a little way along the passage.

"Evening, sir. All quiet."

"So I gather. If Mrs. Howard comes, let her pass —don't show yourself."

"Very good, sir."

"But come up to the door as soon as she's entered."

"Yes, sir."

Roger rang the flat bell. There was a sound of movement immediately, and then a middle-aged woman, sturdy and calm-eyed, opened the door— a policewoman here as a housekeeper. She barred the way, holding the door tightly, until she recognized West. Then she relaxed and gave a smile that betrayed something of her tension.

"Evening, sir."

"How are tricks?" Roger asked.

"Miss Howard's all right," the policewoman said, "I could deal with her kind, but the other one— high horse isn't the word for it."

"She's had a tough time."

"Haven't they both?"

Roger said, "Yes, I suppose so. I'll go and see them. Let Mrs. Howard in, if she comes, then follow her."

The woman opened a door of the drawing room, large and pleasant, with a long window overlooking the Heath. Now the window sill was gay with roses in low metal bowls and sweet peas with their tall stems. The radio was on, tuned low. Norma Dearing was leaning back in an armchair, beating

233

time to the music with her right foot. Regina was sitting upright, knitting.

Both looked round.

Norma jumped to her feet in a flash. It was easy to understand the policewoman's comments; she looked drawn and querulous, and her voice was waspish, "Is there any news? Have you found him?"

"Not yet," Roger said. "I hope—"

"Oh, you *hope*," Norma sneered, and turned away; but there were tears in her beautiful blue eyes, and Roger could sense her tension, her despair.

But he wasn't really interested in Norma. He watched Regina, had taken more notice of her from the beginning. She was tired, too, there were the same signs of tension, but her voice was more controlled.

"How can we help you, Mr. West?"

Did she know the truth? Did she even suspect that her mother had any part in this? Nothing in her clear eyes suggested that, nothing in her face or manner hinted that it was possible.

"I want to know a little more about Dickerson, if you can recall anything," Roger said. "More about his earlier association with your mother."

"But I've told you everything I can." That answer seemed so honest. "He was really a friend of my father, although hardly a familiar, but after the lapse of years Mother and he became quite friendly."

"Just quite friendly?"

She looked puzzled; not frightened or alarmed, but bewildered.

"Well, yes, that's all. I—"

The telephone bell rang.

Roger moved toward the instrument quickly. Both girls sensed that this was no ordinary call and no routine visit. Norma, who had dropped back into her chair, stood up very slowly, tensely.

Roger said, "West speaking."

"Mrs. Howard's on her way up, sir," a policeman said, breathless with excitement. "We let her come, as you said."

"Yes, good." It wasn't easy to be matter of fact. "I'll be down in a few minutes." That would mislead the two girls. "Just stand by."

"Yes, sir."

Roger put down the receiver. The girls, standing close together, watched him with increasing tension. He tried to break it by questioning Regina again, and bringing Derek Talbot into the theme. He didn't ease his own or their tension much.

Then the front door bell rang.

They heard a woman's voice.

The drawing-room door opened, and the policewoman appeared first, barring the older woman's way.

"It's Mrs. Howard, sir."

"Mrs. *who?*" Roger believed that he made himself sound as astonished as he wanted Regina to believe that he was; and he watched her intently.

He was quite sure that she was astounded. It showed in the way her mouth opened, then closed, in the way her eyes rounded. Then she recovered, and moved forward swiftly.

"Mummy!"

"Hallo, dear," Mrs. Howard said. She came in, dressed in a suit of dark gray and with a neat little felt hat without a veil. "I thought I'd come and see how you were getting on." She gave her rather vague smile. "I must say it looks very nice and comfortable here, the kind of place you ought to have, I think. Don't you, dear? I always hoped you would have somewhere like this when you won that competition. I'm sure you would have won, aren't you, if it weren't for this unhappy business? Although I must say you're very pretty, dear, too." She turned to Norma Dearing, gave a vague little smile, and stood looking about her.

Roger waited tensely.

"I'd love a cup of tea, now I'm here," Mrs. Howard said suddenly. "Do you think you could get me one, Gina? It's rather a long way." She gave a tired smile, and her lips were blue-tinged. Regina looked alarmed.

"Yes, of course, Mother. Come and sit down. I'll get—"

She helped her mother into a chair.

To Roger, it was an anticlimax which almost hurt. The woman with half her normal face sat down, gasped, settled back comfortably, and then took out a small bottle. It held two or three brown tablets.

"I'd better have one of these," she said, then took something else out of her handbag; a small packet of sweets. "Would you like a peppermint, dear?"

"You know I don't like them, Mother," Regina said. "Perhaps Norma—"

Mrs. Howard proffered the packet to Norma Dearing.

"Do have one, dear."

"No, I—well, thank you very much."

Norma took one.

Roger moved, and jolted her arm; the pepper-

236

mint dropped. Mrs. Howard didn't seem to notice. She popped one of the brown tablets into her mouth, leaned back and closed her eyes.

Regina was on the way to the kitchen.

Roger picked up the peppermint.

Mrs. Howard gave a funny, gasping sound, and then choked. Roger saw her moving up in her chair, with an awful expression on her face—a look of absolute horror. Then she made another dreadful choking noise, the breath seemed to whistle between her lips, and she dropped back.

She was dying. . . .

There was a smell of bitter almonds; and Roger knew in that dread moment that the brown tablet had contained cyanide of potassium.

There wasn't a chance of saving her, nor a chance of keeping Regina away. She came hurrying back, saw her mother, and stopped, her face blanched.

An hour later, the police knew beyond all doubt that the peppermint that Mrs. Howard had given to Norma Dearing was also filled with cyanide. So were the others in the packet, and the two remaining brown "heart" tablets. The only prints on the packet and the bottle were Mrs. Howard's.

"She knew her daughter didn't like peppermints, so saw just one way to finish Norma off, and put an end to her own life," Sergeant Dalby said, heavily. "She must have been properly at the end of her tether. What a case and what a motive! To get rid of all those lovely girls, just to make sure her own daughter would win—"

He broke off.

Chatworth said gruffly, "I don't understand it.

237

Surely she must have known that before many of the Queens were dead, the Competition would be suspended, even if it wasn't canceled. It may seem the only motive, but it doesn't satisfy *me*."

"At most it's a part of the motive," Roger declared.

He startled them both. They turned to stare.

"Do you mind if we have Dickerson in, sir?" Roger asked. "I'd like to get his reaction when he knows that Mrs. Howard's dead." He was stony-faced; and Chatworth didn't raise any argument, but sent for Dickerson.

The little man came in, diffidently. He kept rubbing his hands together, and it was obvious that they were strong hands, large in proportion to the length of his arms.

Roger told him....

His face puckered. He didn't actually cry, but looked as if he would break down at any moment. He backed toward a chair, groped for it, and sat down.

He found his voice.

"I was—afraid she'd do something like that," he muttered. "Ever since I discovered what she was doing. I—I loved her so much. I didn't want to betray her. I knew she was very ill, even close to death, I hoped—I hoped she would die before the truth came out." He drew a hand across his eyes, and when he took it away his eyes were misty. "The accident must have turned her mind, of course. She was so very beautiful. And Regina was like her—if anything, even lovelier. She longed for Regina to win this Competition, it was her one remaining desire. But—" He caught his breath, screwed up his eyes, and went on almost inaudi-

238

bly: "To think she could plan to kill all those lovely girls, it—it doesn't bear thinking about. Poor Regina, she—"

"Dickerson," Roger broke in, "why did you go to St. Cleo's Vicarage on the night of Betty Gelibrand's murder?"

Dickerson's head jerked up. "Eh? Why did I—but I didn't! It's a lie to say that I went there, I haven't been near St. Cleo's for years. Years!"

Roger said harshly, "Sure?"

"Of course I'm sure!"

"Well, your fingerprints were found there," Roger said very gently. "Yours and Millsom's. How did you persuade Millsom to meet you there?"

Dickerson gaped.

"Let's have the truth," Roger said roughly. "Lying won't help you. How did you persuade Harold Millsom to leave home and meet you at St. Cleo's? How did you lure him up onto the roof? How did you manage to suffocate and then kill him with those strangler's hands of yours?"

"It—it's a lie! It's a wicked lie!"

"We know all about it," Roger rasped. "We know why you wanted to kill the girls, and we know you built up a cover behind Mrs. Howard. You wore her clothes, lured her out when you wanted to make sure she had no alibi, and she was so biddable and grateful to you. Even when you were suspected of the murders, it didn't occur to her that you were guilty. And you—you disappeared, but were all ready to say it was for her sake, weren't you? You thought she could be killed before she could deny anything, but the way you fixed it was not quite clever enough. Too desperate, Dickerson. We also know—"

"But why should I want to kill those girls, those lovely girls?" cried Dickerson. "Why should I want to strike them down in the full bloom of their beauty? Why—"

"Just words," Roger said brusquely; and Chatworth and Dalby seemed to be as much dumbstruck as Dickerson. "You weren't interested in the girls. You could take their measurements and do it all quite indifferently, couldn't you? Beauty didn't mean a thing. But Conway's did. You hated Conway's. You believed they'd cheated you out of your business, and you wanted your own back. And you'd brooded over that for thirty years scheming ways of getting revenge."

Dickerson opened his mouth as if to scream; but the sound wouldn't come out.

Roger went on very quietly, "And then this Competition began to bring Conway's in better business than they'd ever known. You had to help, too; and it nearly drove you mad. You searched desperately, crazily, for a way of damaging the business, getting your own back, hurting Conway's. Then you saw a way to do it while killing beautiful girls. Since Mrs. Howard's accident you've resented beauty, but beauty gave you a spurious motive, one to fool us. Osborn or Talbot might be suspected of trying to clear the way for Regina, but not you. Oh, no, you were quite safe. You worked on both men, and made a final effort to show that it was Talbot, trying to make him visit the girls. When that didn't work, you had a last chance—to blame Mrs. Howard."

Dickerson's mouth was working.

Roger growled to Chatworth, "That's the case,

sir. It was Dickerson from the beginning. When I realized that ever since Conway's bought him out he's been resentful, I glimpsed the real motive: to hurt Conway's. Add his hatred of beauty because of what had happened to Mrs. Howard, and it becomes cold-bloodedly logical. We'll find that he used Millsom as a cover in the beginning. He probably meant to make Betty Gelibrand the last victim. Then it really began to hurt Conway's, and they started squealing. So he went on. In a last effort to save himself he primed Mrs. Howard, told her to go and see Regina, gave her poisoned peppermints, poisoned 'heart' tablets. Sooner or later she'd die. It would look like suicide, Dickerson hoped—and with luck she'd be in or near the girls' flat—as if on the way to kill Regina's only rival. He'll hang, of course, we won't have any trouble in—"

Comfortable, stolid Sergeant Dalby moved swift as a cat, to snatch at Dickerson's hand as he carried something to his mouth. It was another cyanide tablet.

They found a store of the poison, bought to kill wasps, beneath a floorboard in his room at Nettle Street.

The answers to the questions which most harassed Roger came after Dickerson broke down. Dickerson had been on the Common watching Betty Gelibrand when she had quarreled with Millsom. He'd awaited his chance, killed her, then gone to see Millsom, knowing his great distress of mind. He'd persuaded Millsom to go to the Vicarage; gone to see him, told him of Betty's death, and said—a long while before it was true—that the police were

241

after Millsom. He had persuaded Millsom to hide in the hut built in the scaffolding, waited for him to fall asleep, then strangled him; and later thrown him to his death.

He had fired at Roger because he had needed time to climb round the scaffolding, while hidden from below, and so get away on the other side of the church. Then he had waited, seen the results, and perfected his scheme to masquerade as a woman wearing Mrs. Howard's clothes, which fitted him reasonably well.

He had wanted more publicity so as to hurt Conway's; and sent the poisoned chocolates, to make the case flare up again. Those sent to Regina, he said, had contained too little arsenic to do her much harm. He appeared to have been genuinely fond of Regina; and by faking an attack on her, sending her poisoned chocolates as well as the explosive letter with its threat, had believed that he had drawn the suspicions of the police away from her.

He said that he had heard Turnbull telling Mrs. Howard of Regina's address.

Turnbull, Roger knew now, had suspected Mrs. Howard from the time a woman had been reported after Barbara Kelworthy's death. He had let her know the address, expecting her to go to the Putney flat, ready to catch her.

Derek Talbot had had different fears: that Regina was guilty.

Talbot had gone to Mrs. Howard's house, searching for the gray suit and the veil. He had picked up a key which Regina had once dropped, and kept it, so that he could get into her house if he felt disposed. That had been weeks ago, before the trouble. He'd found the little gray hat with the black-blobbed veil, and Turnbull had arrived and found him with it.

Talbot had tried to get away, Turnbull had stopped him, they'd fought, and Turnbull had knocked Talbot out, leaving him with a bloody mouth and nose; and got his own clothes bloodstained.

Dickerson had been hiding in the house, heard all this, entered the room when Talbot was coming round, been recognized—and made that murderous attack. But he had been desperately afraid of being caught red-handed, heard Mrs. Howard at the front door, and run off before Talbot was dead.

Some time later, Talbot had come round enough to scrawl that sentence. The bloodstains on his sleeve meant that he had collapsed before he finished, and smeared the vital last word.

Turnbull, still sullen, had been released, and was under suspension for the attack on Roger and while the Yard probed into his conduct during the case. Roger had the probing to do, and a recommendation to make. He didn't like it, but was shaken when, three days after the case was over, with Talbot out of danger and Regina Howard over the worst of her grief, he had a call from Turnbull's bank manager.

"My client left a letter here for me to pass on to you, Mr. West. I'm sending it by special messenger."

"Do you know what's in it?" Roger asked, almost incredulous.

"I'm afraid not."

"When was it left with you?"

"About a week ago," the manager said. "The date is on the envelope."

The date was the day following Roger's talk with the Vicar of St. Cleo's; when he had challenged Turnbull to find something else of significance in his report of the interview.

The contents of the letter were very brief:

Interview with St. Cleo's Parson

Missed motive—Dickerson hates Conway's guts. Better one than we've had so far, isn't it?

W.T.

Roger took it along to Chatworth.

Chatworth grunted.

"All right, I know he has his bright moments. That doesn't make him a good policeman. I'll think about it, Roger."

At least that took the responsibility off Roger's shoulders.

Roger was in the front room at the Bell Street house when a car pulled up outside. It was late evening, ten days later. The boys were in bed, Janet was in the kitchen, preparing a snack for supper. Roger heard the footsteps along the drive, firm and heavy. He went to the door.

The hall light shone on Turnbull.

Turnbull said, "Mind if I talk to you?" in a steely

244

voice; obviously he was ready for a rebuff.

"Why, hallo," Roger said easily. "Come in, Warren." He stood aside, and, looking away from Turnbull's startled face, called out, "Jan, make another sandwich or so, Warren Turnbull's looked in."

They went into the front room.

They had met two or three times since the arrest of Dickerson, who was now awaiting trial with no hope of saving his life. Turnbull was still under suspension, and Chatworth hadn't yet made it known what he proposed to do.

Turnbull looked massive and boldly handsome; he was taken aback by the amiable welcome, as much as by the smile on Roger's face.

"We usually have tea," Roger said, "but if you'd rather have a drink—"

"Er—well, thanks. Is there whisky?" Turnbull waited until the glass was in his hand, and then gave an unexpected grin; a fierce one. "I need something to steady my nerves! I want some advice. You're the experienced copper, the right man to give it to me."

"Try me," Roger invited.

"Okay. First of all you'd better know that Regina and I are likely to get married. We shall if I know anything about it. Talbot's accepted his *congé*. Regina's a bit nervous of me, but she'll get over that."

So he was as dominating as ever.

"I should make sure she's over it before you get married," Roger said dryly. "Or isn't that the subject you want advice on?"

Turnbull grinned again. "You know damned well it's not. Listen, Handsome. I expect to be

245

drummed out of the Yard. I could resign, that would make it easier all round, but I don't like the idea. But I will—if you think I ought to. I know you well enough to be pretty sure you'll judge on the one thing that matters—whether I'll make a good cop or not. Think I will?"

"I think you could," Roger said judicially. He lit a cigarette—and then realized that Turnbull's was Virginian. That was quite a gesture. "I don't think I should want to work with you too often, I've a feeling we'd always clash, but I'd be sorry to think you were off the Force."

"I think that's all I want to hear," Turnbull said, in a much softer voice than usual.

"It isn't quite all you're going to hear," Roger said. "The Yard can put the bar up, if they want to, but I think they'll take advice. My advice would have to be that although you took too much into your own hands on the Beauty Queens job, the only time you went badly wrong was at St. Cleo's. I should tell Chatworth that I think you ought to be demoted from Inspector, and have a year or so as Detective Sergeant. That," Roger went on very deliberately, "is what I say to you, too." He waited, but no outburst came. "Because I can't very well risk having you on my heels, jostling me out of the way, can I?" he added. "The only way I can keep you under my thumb is to keep you down."

His eyes were smiling.

There was an understanding glow in Turnbull's.

"What the hell difference do you think a year or two is going to make? I'll catch up and pass you before you're really awake! I—Handsome." Turnbull dropped a hand on Roger's shoulder. "Try to fix it, will you? I think the Old Man will listen to you. I'll start from the ranks again if needs be." His big fingers bit into Roger's flesh. "Will you?"

"If I can," Roger promised.

Two days later he was briefing Detective Sergeant Turnbull about a job in the East End.

By the year 2000, 2 out of 3 Americans could be·illiterate.

It's true.

Today, 75 million adults...about one American in three, can't read adequately. And by the year 2000, U.S. News & World Report envisions an America with a literacy rate of only 30%.

Before that America comes to be, you can stop it...by joining the fight against illiteracy today.

Call the Coalition for Literacy at toll-free **1-800-228-8813** and volunteer.

**Volunteer
Against Illiteracy.
The only degree you need
is a degree of caring.**

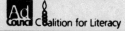